VALERIE NORRIS

Beyond Closure

Published by
Llyfrau Cambria Books, Wales, United Kingdom.
Cambria Books is a division of
Cambria Publishing.
Discover our other books at: www.cambriabooks.co.uk

For my husband, Christopher Norris, with my heartfelt thanks for all his help and support.

CONTENTS

Chapter 1

You knew it was going to be a hot day when commuters headed for the train in their shirtsleeves at eight-thirty in the morning. I joined them, jacket dangling across my shoulder from my finger. No tie; Neville was encouraging more relaxed attire in the practice. It puts the clients at ease and helps them to trust in us, he had explained earnestly at one of our new team meetings. Even a smart T-shirt and jeans would not be going too far. I could see what he was getting at, but after ten years of hiding behind my collar and tie uniform I needed to take the journey towards smart casual in stages.

The train glided slowly onto the platform. One thing about living near the end of the line, you could almost always get a seat. We didn't actually go underground either, which was another blessing. It was only five stops anyway, hardly time to check your messages or read *The Guardian* headlines on your phone. Not many people got off at my stop; most of them were bound for the increasing madness that was Central London.

I do count my blessings that I have such an easy commute. A fairly short walk after I leave the train, down leafy avenues. And it was only one change and about forty minutes to get to Lisa's, either from home or from work, and much the same to get to Cora's. A golden triangle in a pretty golden life.

I entered my code into the keypad next our main door. A welcome coolness enveloped me. Lucy, telephone to her ear, mouthed hello and gave a small wave from where she sat at the reception desk. I picked up the post from the tray at the end of her desk, idly leafing through the circulars and other junk that mainly came in the regular mail nowadays. I half-paid attention to her 'oh dears' and other expressions of sympathy, ending with 'thanks for letting us know and I hope you'll feel better soon'. I liked Lucy. She managed to get the right amount of calmness and reassurance into her voice, essential for dealing with our vulnerable clients, and she also managed to keep all our admin afloat with minimal errors. Quite a feat for someone in her twenties. It also didn't hurt that I found her easy on the eye; smiley with just a hint of cleavage and thigh on show. And yes, I know I shouldn't even have noticed. I just hoped that Neville was aware of her good work and had given her a pay rise.

'That was Emma,' she said. 'She has a tummy bug, throwing up all night and everything, so she can't come in.' She frowned and pulled up a screen on her computer.

'Does she have any bookings this morning?'

'First one ten o'clock. New client. She was already waiting on the doorstep when I opened up a few minutes ago. I put her in the waiting room.' She looked at me with those big brown eyes and a questioning smile and I knew what was coming.

I thought of trying to wriggle out of it. Instead I said, 'I suppose it serves me right for being first in. Anyway, I don't have anything else this morning.'

'You're an angel. It's in Room 1. Oh, and you do have something else this morning – the team meeting.'

I groaned. 'I knew there was a reason I didn't like Mondays.'

Room 1 was in its customary good order, plain and tasteful with minimal distractions and adornments, yet not seeming spartan. Walls a muted beige with a single picture hung of the blurry modern type you get in hotel bedrooms. Two low chairs faced each other across a coffee table, upon which a box of tissues stood conveniently. A couple of china figurines and a vase of flowers sat on a side table. Traffic from the main road a couple of streets away was a mere low hum. It was my favourite counselling room.

It wasn't yet ten o'clock but I thought I might as well make a start, since she had taken the trouble to get here so early. I allowed my body to go loose and made sure I had a welcoming expression pasted on my face before I opened the door.

'Miriam Wallace?' She was hunched in a corner seat, middle

2

aged with grey hair and beseeching eyes, nervousness and anguish etched into every part of her body. I invited her in.

'I booked to see a woman counsellor,' she said, not moving.

I introduced myself and explained that unfortunately Emma had been taken ill but that I would be happy take her place just for today. Eventually I cajoled her to move into the counselling room. She sat down gingerly on the edge of her seat, her handbag clutched on her lap. I chattered away gently, hoping that would allow her to settle down, enquiring about her journey and explaining that first there were just a few forms to fill in.

She eyed me suspiciously. 'I read about the other lady on the Internet. She sounded nice. I'm not sure about this.'

'I'm really sorry about the sudden change. Now that you're actually here perhaps we could fill the forms in and make a start?'

She made no move to take a form so I said, 'Why don't I kick off by telling you something about myself. My first degree is in psychology and I have a Masters degree too. I've been in this practice for ten years. I specialise in bereavement but I've got plenty of experience in other areas too.'

'I don't want someone that qualified. I only want someone to talk to. It will cost more with you, won't it?' Her voice was rising. I reassured her as best I could. Poor woman, I thought. Poor frightened woman. Eventually she said she would rather leave and come back when she could see Emma. There was nothing more I could do.

I sat on in the counselling room after she had left. Then I stirred myself and put the encounter aside. Coffee, my body was saying. Coffee to fortify myself for the upcoming team meeting. As I went back to reception Lucy called to me, 'There was a message for you on the answerphone, left over the weekend. I've sent it on to your mobile.'

I went into the staff room and unlocked my drawer to get my work mobile out. I pressed the button and listened. I recognised the voice, breathy and soft, in two seconds flat.

This is a message for Simon. I lost your mobile number, so I hope you

3

get this. I need to see you again. You see, he's come back.

*

Everyone except Neville was assembled when I got to the meeting. By the time I had exchanged greetings with the others, poured myself a large mug of black coffee from the jug waiting on the hotplate and grabbed a couple of chocolate biscuits – the best thing about the meeting – Neville had come in with a man in tow whom I hadn't met. He had brown hair down onto his shoulders, a medium length beard and he was wearing a loose, brightly coloured shirt. More like a kaftan, really. So this was the heralded new boy. Well, he certainly seemed to be embracing the casual dressing ethos.

Neville opened his notebook and smiled his welcome at all of us.

After the preliminaries he said, 'I'm very pleased to be able to welcome the newest member of The Willows team. May I introduce Kai to you all, who is going to add the specialism of hypnotherapy to enhance our range of services.'

We introduced ourselves round the table, then Neville explained to him that he had introduced these monthly meetings for group sharing between us therapists – in confidence, of course - as well as to transact any business of the practice. Kai nodded enthusiastically from time to time, to show he was paying attention, and only spoke when asked a question, in acceptable newbie fashion. When asked by Neville to tell us all something about his experience and what he believed that hypnotherapy could bring to The Willows Psychotherapy Services, he pulled out a scribbled sheet of notes from his pocket and referred to that, stumbling over his words now and again. Neville kept his rictus of a smile in place and beamed round the room every now and again. I buried myself in my coffee and ate my second biscuit.

It had got to the bit where we were going round the table and given a chance to 'highlight any issues of interest' that we

4

wanted to share with the group. Neville liked the word 'share'. He and everyone else listened to my few anodyne sentences about my caseload.

'Thank you, Simon. Succinct, as ever.' Then, as if it were an afterthought, he said, 'Oh by the way, there was a message for you on the answerphone. Did Lucy send it on to you?'

'Yes. She did.'

'Good, good. Is this an ongoing client? It was quite a cryptic message.'

I kept my voice pleasantly neutral. 'I had several sessions with her nearly a year ago. The sessions were terminated by the client's wishes.'

'Ah, a follow up. Well, as you know, it can be helpful in return cases for a different therapist to work with the client, to bring a fresh eye to the situation. As it happens, I have some spaces in my own schedule.'

'No.'

'In the best interests of the client...'

'Thank you, but it's a complex case and in this instance my years of experience tell me that the best interests of this client are served by interaction with someone who has complete knowledge of the background.'

We held each other's eyes, and I could almost hear the collective intake of breath around the table.

The smile didn't waver. 'It's your client, of course. I suggest that you talk it over with your supervisor before making a decision.' He shuffled the papers in front of him. 'And now we come on to this month's accounts...'

*

It was hot in the train and I was strap hanging.

It had been a busy day. So busy, in fact, that I hadn't had time to start re-reading the file as I had intended to. Despite – or more honestly because of – Neville's suggestion I had tried to

5

phone her to make an appointment, but only got the answer machine. It was a different outgoing message to last year. I played it a couple of times. Were there different intonations, nuances? I wasn't sure.

When Neville collared me later in the day I thought it might have been to renew his pressure about a change of therapist for my client, but no. He had asked if I could take Kai under my wing a bit and make him feel at home, seeing as I was the only other bloke in the practice. I didn't mind too much. Kai pulling out some prepared notes and revealing his nervousness in the meeting had rather endeared him to me. And frankly I was curious about him. So he and I arranged to have a drink tomorrow. He eagerly suggested today after work, but I told him I'd already got something on that I couldn't change.

I distracted myself and put the day behind me by looking out of the train window at the houses, back gardens, paddling pools, sunbeds and barbeques that trundled by. Being 'in the moment,' as they say. I wondered if Kai used that in his sessions? Perhaps you don't with hypnotherapy. I don't know enough about these things.

I was relieved to leave the sultriness of the train behind to walk the half mile to Lisa's house. It was at the far end of a cul-de-sac, which rather had the effect of squashing the gardens at the bottom of the street and giving the houses the appearance of overcrowded teeth in a mouth. The gate to the front garden hung tipsily from its hinges and screeched across the path as I pushed it open. I thought for the umpteenth time that I could take the gate off and rehang it properly for her. One day. I picked my way through the tangle of the garden to the back door, which was wide open. The bubbling smell of lasagne drifted out, very welcome because I hadn't managed to grab much for lunch. Lisa was bending over the washing machine, stuffing towels and miscellaneous garments inside. Once upon a time I would have playfully smacked her bottom.

She heard me and straightened up, her hair partly coming

adrift from where she had it piled on the top of her head.

'Hello,' she said, rescuing her hair and jabbing a hairpin into it. 'God, it's hot.' She leant towards me and we swapped perfunctory kisses on the cheek. She was still pinning her hair up and I caught a whiff of her armpit. I reminded myself that she didn't have the benefit of working in an air-conditioned environment like I did. I supposed that the local schools had to make do with a fan in the staff room.

'And you've been slaving over a hot stove. Or at least it smells like it.' I followed her into the kitchen and hung my jacket on the chairback.

She half-heartedly gestured towards the kettle. 'Coffee? Or there's some lager in the fridge.' I made the obvious choice and we sat at the kitchen table with our cold cans.

'Where's the boys?'

She lifted her eyes upwards. 'The usual. Nathan's in his bedroom doing his homework. Or so he says. 'And Joe's playing games on his tablet. Same old same old. I don't get much out of either of them when I come in. I'd rather you left Nath up there until teatime so he doesn't have any excuses not to finish his homework.'

I looked at her appraisingly over the rim of my beer can. She was carrying a bit too much weight, but then she always had, and I thought it suited her. Yet today there seemed to be a droopiness about her.

'You seem a bit down. Is everything OK? It's not unusual for kids to behave like that nowadays, you know.'

'What's this, a free counselling session?'

'No, I'm just concerned.'

'Well, you don't need to be. I'm just hot and bothered and I can't wait for the term to finish. Not long now. What's happening in your life?'

This was always difficult, given that she didn't want to hear much about Cora and there was so much confidentiality connected with my work. And what else did I do, really, apart

7

from my cycling, which also didn't interest her? So I always glossed over this one and we ended up talking about Nathan and Joe, which is why I was there, after all.

While Lisa was getting the lasagne out of the oven I volunteered to fetch the boys for their tea. I called hello to Joe, who was cross-legged on the sofa immersed in his tablet with a frown of concentration. He didn't reply. Upstairs Nathan's bedroom door was closed. He didn't respond to my knock and I thought, correctly, that he must be wearing headphones. I put my head cautiously around the door and there he was, sprawled on his back on the bed, phone in hand, thumbs flying over the screen. He didn't see me straightaway. Somehow he seemed even longer and lankier lying down. I moved into the room and he registered that it was me. 'Dad!' he said, his face lighting up immediately into a big grin. All thoughts of enquiring about his homework went out of my head.

*

Tea hadn't got off to the best start. We had gone into the living room to summon Joe, but despite my greeting him a couple of times he hadn't replied but stayed glued to the screen.

'Joe!' said Nathan. 'Come on, say hello to Simon.'

Before I could stop him Nathan had grabbed the tablet and taken it right out of Joe's hands. There then followed a sustained screeching from Joe, the kind that makes you want to cover your ears. Lisa bustled in and demanded to know what was happening, and so the pandemonium continued, now extending to a squabble between her and Nathan as to how he should have known better than to interfere with Joe. Eventually Joe was calmed down and we all subsided round the kitchen table. God, I thought, she puts up with this every day.

The excellent lasagne followed by ice cream mollified us all. I tried some light conversation with Nathan about school and what he was doing with his mates, and he replied politely but uninformatively, like he tended to when his mother was around. Not that he ever told me everything, I'm sure, but there were times when we were on our own together, usually in front of the telly at mine eating a pizza, when he would open up. I allowed myself to be persuaded, in those times, that he was a pretty normal fourteen-year-old kid and that I had managed not to screw him up too badly.

Joe concentrated on his food and so I let him. Lisa had asked me not to mention their forthcoming caravan holiday because it might bring on his anxiety. Already he had asked her about what his bed would be like, where they would eat and could he bring his tablet and his drawing things. She knew there might be challenges with him, but she said she was yearning for a holiday. I agreed. She needed a break.

'Joe,' said Lisa when we had all finished the last of the ice cream, 'Are you going to fetch the picture that you've drawn for Simon?' Without a word he slid off his chair and padded off to his room, coming back with a sheet from his drawing book, which he gave to me. 'It's for you,' he said. 'It's a city.'

It took me a while to take in the intricate lines and shadings of the tall buildings, the well-judged proportions and the flow of the river in the foreground. 'Wow,' was all I could say. 'Joe, this is really very good. Thank you so much. I don't know how you do it.'

'I just draw what I see,' he said. 'It's easy.'

I continued to gaze at the picture. I wanted to show it to Cora and get her to evaluate it. Surely Joe had talent that should be nurtured. I tentatively held up my hand to him for a high five. Today I was lucky and got one back.

*

Later on the train, I pulled out my work phone. This time I got an answer.

9

Chapter 2

The file was substantial. I pulled it out from the filing cabinet and sat down at the table in the staff room to open it. On the cover sheet I read

Name: Fleur Bentley. Age: 32

My eyes flicked over other information on the cover sheet such as address, doctor's details, any medication and reasons for consultation. So, it had been last year that I had first met Fleur Bentley. She had probably been wearing one of her long, flowing skirts, although looking back I'm not sure. What I do remember definitely is her delicate, fluttering hands, her soft, high-pitched voice and, of course, her hair. You wouldn't forget that.

I turned the pages and read the notes on our first and second sessions. Then – and this was why the case file was bulky – as well as my own copious case notes there were Fleur's notes, written in her own handwriting. I remembered how she had been struggling to articulate her backstory to me in words, so I had suggested that she might want to write it down instead. And this had worked; after she had got into the swing of it she had produced page after page in her curly, flowing script. I flicked through the pages. I needed to study all this again carefully before I saw her in just over two weeks' time.

When I phoned she had answered on the second ring with a cautious 'Hello?'

'Can I speak to Fleur Bentley,' I said, even though I was pretty certain it was the voice that I remembered.

She confirmed that it was her and I told her it was Simon from The Willows Psychotherapy Services, returning her call. I asked her how she was.

'I'd like to make an appointment to see you again. I don't

suppose you have anything in the next couple of days?'

I grimaced. I knew the rest of this week was choc-a-block. I offered her next week but she told me she was going away for a week with the whole of her family to celebrate her parents' ruby wedding. If it were really urgent, I could enquire among my colleagues I said reluctantly. No, she'd rather wait and see me, she said, because I knew her background and she trusted me. She trusted me. In your face, Neville.

And so it was arranged. I felt reassured that she would be with her family in the meantime. Even though I was curious, I knew better than to lift the lid now without the time and space to deal with it fully, which always did more harm than good.

I had nearly finished reading my notes on the first two sessions when Stacey came into the staff room, all beads and dangling earrings.

'Oh, hello Simon. How are you?' She delved into the cupboard and emerged with an open pack of chocolate biscuits. 'I'm starving. No time for breakfast this morning.'

'Good, thanks.' I waved away the gaping pack that she was offering me. 'And you?' I hoped she wouldn't want any more than this conventional exchange, but she had punctured open a carton of juice and drawn up a seat at the table.

'I thought you and Neville were going to have a stand-up row at the meeting yesterday. But that round went to you, I think.' Her voice was muffled through the biscuit chewing. 'Quite right, too. He shouldn't poke his nose in like he does. You're perfectly capable.' Her earrings, which nearly touched her shoulders, swung wildly with her indignation.

Stacey was always one to fight a corner, be it her own or other people's. I knew she was a committed member of Greenpeace and Friends of the Earth. Our very own young activist. You need a few people like that.

'To be honest, I haven't thought about it since. I've been busy.'

'And you are going to see your old client again, I hope?'

'Yes. As it happens I've just booked it. I'm starting re-reading the notes now.'

'Is that the file? Shit, it's big! How long were you seeing her for? Ten years?'

'No, just a few weeks actually.'

Stacey straightened out the empty biscuit packet and tipped it back into her mouth to get the last of the crumbs. Half of them missed the target and scattered down her front, getting trapped in the beads. 'Well, I'm off. I've got an interesting one coming up – intrigue, lies, family breakdown, the lot.'

Another ten minutes went by as I assimilated what was there in the case notes. I realised that I didn't have much time now to start getting into Fleur's narrative. Instead I flicked through the pages of my records of our sessions until I got to the final one. I remembered that final one very clearly, without having to refer to the notes in front of me.

I also remembered that day for another reason. That evening was the first time I slept with Cora.

*

My name is Fleur Bentley. I am 32 years old. Simon asked me to write about myself, but I'm not sure what he wants me to put, or where he wants me to start. From my childhood, I suppose. When I think back, Mom and Dad didn't used to talk very much. I have a brother a few years older than me, but he was always off with his own friends, so my memory of my childhood is that it usually seemed quiet in our house.

I wasn't named after anyone special or anything. Mom had just read the name Fleur in a book years ago and it had stuck in her mind, she said. I didn't have a middle name.

I always liked school. I suppose I liked learning and I liked the routine. I had several friends and I went on holiday every year with my parents and brother. I can't think of anything else to say about my childhood.

I went to university when I was eighteen, after school. It took me a while to settle in. It was all so different. I suppose I was homesick. But then

I got used to being in a new city, I made a few friends and I got on well with my course. It was Maths. I came out with a good degree, I got a job in a firm of accountants and I've been here in West London ever since. Ten years now.

Well, that's my past life in a nutshell. I don't know if Simon wants me to write more than that? He said to just write whatever came into my head about 'my story', but I know what he really wants me to write about. Michael. There. I've said it.

I had to stop for a bit to get some tissues. I can't even write his name without crying. But I must try. If this therapy is going to help me at all, I must try. The doctor said it would be a good thing to see a grief counsellor.

So here goes. I first met Michael on a train when I was travelling to work. I wouldn't have described myself as the sort of person who would talk to a strange man on a train, let alone allow myself to get picked up. But it didn't really seem like getting picked up, it was so gradual. We used to travel on the same route, me getting off before him, because he travelled right into the city. I had noticed him in a vague sort of way before, then one day I dropped my book and he picked it up for me. He gave me a warm smile and asked me if it was good. The book, that is. I expect I just mumbled something. Later on he teased me and said that I'd dropped the book on purpose, but I hadn't. After that he would say hello every time he saw me on the train, which was most days. It got to the stage where I would be looking out for him, and we would exchange a few words. I couldn't believe it when one day he asked if I had time for a cup of coffee after work. I said yes and it just went from there.

What shall I say about Michael? He was eight years older than me. He was slim, handsome and sporty. He was always bothered because he was losing his hair, but I never thought that stopped him from being good looking. I can see his picture now, on the wall. It's us on our wedding day. We both look so happy. Oh, Michael, I still can't believe it. I can't write any more now.

*

I got there a few minutes early for the pub session with Kai. We had decided on one of the popular pubs close to the practice. I thought as I settled down with my pint that this sort of pub reminds you of your old-fashioned spit-and-sawdust public bar that my grandad would have drunk in, combined with a twenty-first century take on that venerated British institution. Add to that a menu that includes vegan choices with barista-style beverages laid on, and you have a happy combination, to my mind.

I almost didn't spot Kai when he came in, because he had traded his colourful loose top for a normal tee shirt with 'Legend' emblazoned across the front – if that can be considered normal. His worried look was replaced by one of relief when he saw me. He sat down with his pint and we drank in unison, then looked around the room. 'So,' I began, 'how's it going so far?' I was conscious that I didn't want to sound as if I were interviewing him, supervising him or, God forbid, letting on that Neville had asked me to buddy him.

He nodded. 'Yeah, good. Everybody seems friendly. I've had one client and she's rebooked for next week. I'm only on a freelance basis as yet of course, but Neville is expecting that once it builds up I could get something more permanent. That's fine for now. I've got several clients I'm still seeing elsewhere.' He nodded again. He reminded me of a dog I used to have. The dog didn't nod exactly; it was more tail-thumping. But it was the same earnest eagerness. 'You said you've been there ten years?'

'Man and boy, you could say. I started part-freelance, with a retainer for walk-ins one day and one evening a week. Nowadays I'm full-time on the staff, along with five others. Everyone else is part or fully freelance. That means I hardly ever see external clients anymore, but then, I don't need to now.' I didn't see any reason not to be open with him.

We passed the ball backwards and forwards a bit longer with me in the role of school prefect and him the new kid, while our pints went down. He went to the bar to get refills. I flicked on my phone while he was waiting and saw there was a message from Cora. '*I'd prefer not to have dinner tonight. I'm in the middle of working. Could we meet tomorrow instead? xx*'

I had wiped the frown off my face by the time Kai returned with the glasses. 'Look,' I said, 'Let's not talk shop all the time. What do you do when you're not hypnotising people?'

'It's hypnotherapy, not hypnosis. Basically the aim is to help the client to achieve a trancelike state where their subconscious is receptive to suggestion. But more often the work itself is based on regression therapy to establish the cause of the neurosis and then this is brought to the conscious mind to be dealt with.' For the first time there was a note of quiet firmness and authority in his voice and I felt suitably rebuked. I apologised and said it wasn't a practice I knew much about, and drew him back to his life outside work.

He picked a beermat up and twiddled it. 'It's a bit shit just at present, since you ask. I've been living alone these past six months since my wife upped and left me, taking the lad with her. Oh, there wasn't anyone else. She just said that "I no longer fulfilled her needs". What the fuck is that supposed to mean? And now she's started divorce proceedings.'

He went on to fill me in on the demise of his marriage, and ended up with an apology for going on about it. I said it was OK, I was good at listening. After all, it's what I do. A perky waitress squeezed past me to deliver two sizzling steaks to the table next door. The savoury smell wafted over us.

'That looks good,' said Kai.

'I believe they don't do a bad meal here. Well, I'm free for the evening. Shall we get something?'

His eyes lit up, but cautiously. 'That would be great. But are you sure? Aren't you expected at home?'

I pulled a face and tapped my phone. 'I've just been stood up, mate.'

*

By the time we we'd eaten our steaks – it was steak night in the pub - and put away a bottle of wine we were chatting away like old friends. So much so that Kai said, 'At least you've got a

15

girlfriend, even if she stood you up tonight. Lucky bugger. Been seeing her for long?'

'Good few months now. We see each other about three times a week and it works well. She's an artist, and sometimes she's really into something she's working on, and that comes before anything else. I'm cool with that, though.' I felt that I should justify tonight's no-show.

'An artist, huh? Does she have an artistic temperament?'

Talk about hitting the nail on the head. Flashbacks of broken crockery, yelling and other dramatic outbursts flitted across the screen in my head. 'You could say that. But it does make for an exhilarating ride.' Again, the wish to defend her.

'I'd settle for any sort of ride right now.'

We glugged away at our house wine while we wolfed down our steak dinners and engaged in deep meaningful conversations about the state of the nation, football and then back to our personal lives.

'So what's your previous history, if you've been seeing this one for a year?'

'Intermittent girlfriends for a few years, nothing serious. Then before that...' I paused, then decided that I might as well go for it. 'Before that I got married young. Twenty-one, in fact. But it didn't last.'

Kai nodded and picked some steak from his teeth. 'I thought you had the look of a re-tread about you. Kids?'

'Yeah, two. Well one, actually. That's why we got married in the first place. Lisa got pregnant and I let her mother put pressure on.'

'What do you mean, "*two well one, actually*?" Sounds like a story there.'

I put down my knife and fork on my empty plate. That was an excellent meal. I made a mental note to include this place in the compendium of good hostelries I kept in my head. 'Nathan was born six months after we got married and we went to live with her parents while I tried to study for my finals. You can

16

imagine what that was like.'

Kai gave a series of his fervent nods. I was beginning to think the nods were his trademark. Perhaps that's how he hypnotised people.

'Basically, I couldn't hack it. The responsibility and all that.' I didn't really want to go into details. 'It wasn't my finest hour, leaving Lisa with a toddler. We divorced and went our separate ways. I got to see Nathan every other weekend and Lisa got a flat with Nathan.'

'What's this about kid number two?'

'Ah, kid number two. That's Joe. A few years back Lisa managed to get herself a holiday to Magaluf and leave Nathan with her Mum. He was eight at the time.'

'Was it "Shagaluf" back then?'

'You said it. Bottom line was the place lived up to its name and Lisa came back expecting Joe. Father unknown.'

Kai whistled. No nodding.

'She was never a slag, though. She just overreacted to her pretty crap life and was unlucky.' Why am I feeling the need to protect the women in my life from Kai's judgement? Interesting. 'Well, her life got even more crap because Joe turned out to have special needs. He's autistic. She took it all really hard. Her mother helped practically, but she never let Lisa forget what a disappointment she was. I was settled into my job at The Willows by this time, so I rallied round. I felt sorry for her and, after all, if there was a poor home environment it was going to impact on Nathan. I gave her what money I could and started going round more, and we abandoned this "alternate weekends access" stuff.' I paused, nudged by the memories. 'She changed, though, after Joe was born. She went from being outgoing and bubbly to being a lot more introverted and withdrawn.'

I shut my mouth. The drink was loosening my tongue.

'So you're pretty much bringing up another man's child, and one with difficulties at that? Respect, man.'

I shrugged. I wanted to get out of this conversation. As luck

17

would have it at that moment a smiley young woman approached our table carrying sheaves of paper and pencils and asking if we'd like to take part in the pub quiz. I looked round and saw that the quizmaster was setting up his microphone and several teams were forming at the tables round us.

We decided to have another bottle of wine and give it a go. Why not? Our team was well-named as "The Therapisseds", which Kai thought of. Or was it me? I'm not sure now. What I do remember is that the Therapisseds didn't exactly cover themselves with glory. We had a good run on some of the sports and pop music questions, but geography and history let us down.

We tumbled out from the fug of the pub into the fresh night air, clapping each other on the back and promising to do it again soon.

'G'night, Kai. Great night. See you tomorrow, if you're in.'

'Not tomorrow. Next day. Oh, and by the way…'

I turned back unsteadily to face him.

'Kai's just my professional name. It means restoration or recovery in Japanese. My real name's Rodney.'

Chapter 3

Over the years I've become an old hand at bereavement counselling. I've found my niche working with death; more specifically, its effects on the living who are left behind. So why does it appeal to me? For one thing you are generally going to see some improvement in the client over the course of the sessions. It's immensely rewarding for me to support them on their difficult journey and see them gradually emerging and recovering from their grief. Most of the people that I see have either been involved with traumatic death or, as the text books tell us, they have 'abnormal or complicated grief'. Honestly, some of the cases I've dealt with, you just wouldn't make up - it would seem too far-fetched.

Bewilderment in the eyes, frozen features, stiff posture. These were what most people displayed who came to sit with me in this counselling room for the first time, and Fleur Bentley had been no different. They all have their stories. They struggle to come to terms with the yawning dislocation in their life caused by the death of someone significant to them. And sometimes, because they had taken the considerable step of coming to see a specialist in bereavement counselling, there would be something deeper, some dark secret or anomaly. It would be this great obstacle that was preventing them from processing their feelings. I had wondered what the obstacle was for Fleur Bentley.

She gave me no clues, in that first meeting, about the complication that was compounding her own particular grief. In response to my gentle questioning, she had told me in not much more than a whispered monotone that her husband Michael had died suddenly, age 39, nine months ago. They had been happily married for seven years and had no children.

We sat there together in the muted space of the counselling room, with its neutral walls and sensitive lighting, while I observed her professionally, as I had done with hundreds of other clients. She was tidily presented in a flowing, loose-style dress. Not that I can remember accurately, almost a year later, exactly what she was wearing but that was the sort of thing she always wore. She was a petite woman, childlike almost, and the comfy armchair that she was occupying seemed to swallow her up. Her hair was long, perhaps the longest I had ever seen, and it hung in one plait, thick as my wrist, over her shoulder and down to her lap.

She answered my fact-finding questions, but it was obvious that she found this painful and answered briefly, not volunteering any extra information. I tried to move on to details of what had happened and to find a line of approach to ascertain where she was on her grief journey, but a look of panic came into her eyes, and she bowed her head and started to cry. At first the tears came slowly, then soon she was sobbing uncontrollably. I offered her tissues and silently held the space while the emotion spilled out of her. When the storm had passed she lay back in the chair, exhausted, and whispered how sorry she was, the tissues lying limp in her hands. I told her that it was perfectly alright, in fact good, that she should cry. It was then that I suggested she could try writing down her story, or as much as she could, before we met again. She might find that was helpful. I knew better than to push her any more at that point.

If there was one word that I would have associated with Fleur Bentley at that first meeting, it was 'fragile'. I would need to take it gently. Very gently. My gut and my experience told me that there were lots of missing pieces, and it would take patience to assemble the jigsaw.

I stood up from the desk in the staff room, stretched my stiff shoulders, shuffled together the case notes and replaced them in the filing cabinet. I would have read more, but it was nearly time to meet Cora, and I didn't want to be late.

*

I wasn't late, although she was. Only ten minutes, and she had messaged me to let me know that she was on her way. Perhaps this was a ploy to crank up the suspense, because she had said in her message that she had a surprise for me. While I was waiting I mused on the fact that I valued punctuality, whereas it was not a top priority with Cora. Did that matter, or was it just one of the interesting asymmetries that our relationship seemed to thrive on? God. Analysing yourself was a hazard of my job.

I saw her from across the restaurant, tall and elegant. It was not so hot today and she had one of her diaphanous shawl-type things laid across her shoulders. I stood up and waved to her. The hinted-at surprise was not subtle; her hair had metamorphosed from the usual light brown, fringed and straight style, to her jawline bob being shorn close to her head on one side and a bold streak of fluorescent purple on the other side. There was only going to be one right response here, and I had to get my body language and facial expression onside.

'Wow,' seemed a good start. 'Talk about audacious. That's how to get you yourself noticed!'

She twirled round, her shawl billowing, allowing me to take in the full effect.

'Do you like it? I wanted something that made a statement.' She swung her head from side to side, so I saw on one side the rippling glossy curtain of hair that was (had been?) one of her most attractive features, now shot with purple and juxtaposed with the starkness of the near-shaven other side. Maybe I was just old-fashioned.

I drew her to me and kissed her cheek on the glossy curtain side of her head. She smelt of nice, spicy things, like mulled wine at Christmas. 'You certainly have done that.'

She drew back from me, 'But do you like it?' Her voice, always slightly husky and rich, now vibrated with her excitement. She positively radiated elation. I appraised her again. It wasn't so bad once you got over the shock. She still had that distinctive

21

glamour that had first attracted me.

'It's very you,' I said, as we took our seats across the white tablecloth. 'Quirky, original, enigmatic, but still feminine and beautiful.'

This went down well. 'Thank you, Simon. I'd been toying with the idea for a couple of weeks, and yesterday I had a depressing day, so I thought, I'm going to do it.'

The waiter discreetly slid menus in front of us and took our order for our normal bottle of Merlot.

'A bad day, was it?'

'Oh... nothing unusual. The students got on my nerves. You would think that teaching art in a summer school would make a refreshing change, but in fact it's little different from teaching art to a bunch of mainly apathetic teens the rest of the year round. They're just a bit older, that's all.'

I reached across the table and squeezed her hand. 'Poor you. Never mind, you've got most of September off, and we'll have our holiday together.'

'It's all very well for you. You love your job.'

I withdrew my hand and opened the menu. 'Yes, it's true. I do.' At that moment the wine arrived. Good. That would help. We clinked glasses in a toast. 'To art. *Your* art.' We both sipped and savoured the first mouthful. 'How's it going, by the way?'

'Really well.' And she told me about her latest painting. I listened, but as ever I was out of my depth when it came to any useful comments. 'That's why I hope you didn't mind that I stayed at home to work last night,' she finished.

I told her that it was fine and entertained her between mouthfuls of our food by recounting my evening out with Kai-Rodney. Cora followed the story eagerly, laughing at our lads' antics. By the time we came to the end of the meal all her slight petulance had evaporated and was replaced by her kittenish charm. I shouldn't really criticise. I can understand that having to earn her living teaching bored art students was a pain when what she really wanted to be doing was producing her own work.

In the back of the Uber she slid her hand into mine and curled her fingers to stroke my palm in a way that I recognised and my pulse quickened. You could never take anything for granted with this woman. She led the way into her high rise flat and turned on three lamps in the living room. This was enough light to see by, but it mercifully downplayed the piles of books, magazines, stacked canvases, dirty coffee cups and miscellanea.

She opened the balcony doors and we stepped out into the sultry night of the suburbs, a mesh of street and car lights glimmering below us.

I slipped my arm around her and she put her head on my shoulder while we absorbed the view.

'Coffee and a nightcap?'

I kissed her before I answered. 'Brandy then. But just a small one. I'll make the coffee if you like. Decaf?'

The lights in the kitchen were a harsh shock after the dimness of the balcony. There was the usual overspill of clutter on all the surfaces – unopened mail, a fruit bowl with trailing bunches of grapes, various pottery artefacts. And I did like the way she had various jars of dried foodstuffs – pasta, lentils, sunflower seeds and suchlike – displayed for their visual appeal rather than their storage efficacy, as she had told me when I first remarked on them back in our early days. As I waited for the kettle to boil I reflected on the difference between Cora's kitchen and Lisa's. Both were small and untidy, but somehow Cora's was a studied effect, a jumble of colours and shapes, whereas Lisa's was the detritus of two boys and a busy life. I let the water go off the boil before I poured it into the cups. By comparison my own kitchen is pretty spartan, mainly because not much happens in there. I do wash up every day though, which is not bad for a bloke. Maybe I could write a paper on what the state of your kitchen reveals about you. Get a grip, Simon.

Back in her living room I cleared a space on the sofa and sat with my brandy glass swirling in my palm. Cora was sitting in the armchair opposite me, her bare feet curled under her. She pulled her earrings off and put them on the side table.

'Have you had any more thoughts about our holiday?' I said.

She took a few seconds to answer. 'Not really. There's so much to choose from.'

'Well, let's narrow it down. One week or two? Home or abroad? We should get something booked soon. Unless you want to go last minute.'

I knew what the real question was, of course. Were we ready for this? We'd never been more than two or three nights with each other.

Cora put her hand up to twiddle a lock of hair; a characteristic gesture. She realised that she had got the shaven side and transferred her attentions to the other side. It really was disconcerting, this lopsided hairdo.

'Cora?'

She took a slow mouthful of her brandy. 'We don't have to decide now, do we? It's late.'

I held her gaze. Her fingers had moved to the side of her neck, which she was stroking. Every gesture, every look was a tease and an invitation now. I thought of the picture rolled up in my bag, Joe's cityscape drawing, which I had intended showing to her when we got back to her flat to get her opinion on his potential. But not now.

*

My second session with Fleur Bentley had been exactly a week after the first one. She had carried into the counselling room with her a sheaf of A4 pages, and I had realised this was her response to my suggestion that she should write down her story. She had slid them out from the plastic sleeve she was carrying and put them on the coffee table between us, next to the box of tissues.

I reread the case notes that I had written for that session. They said that she was more composed on the second occasion than on the first, although she looked tired and pale. Not that I needed to reread it, there in black and white in my own handwriting, to be reminded of that. I read on.

When I asked her how she'd been, she told me that work had been busy but she had found time in the evenings and weekend to write, and that once she had got into it she found it came quite easily. I asked if she wanted me to read it now, and she did. I explained that I would read it quite quickly, so as not to take up valuable time in the session, and study it in more depth later on.

The account contained details of her courtship and subsequent life with Michael. It became more factual and historic as she wrote, and less focussed on her anguish at his loss. She sang his praises constantly, often dwelling on his athletic prowess, kindness and other admirable features. There were descriptions of holidays and other good times that they had shared. Clearly there was a great deal of idealisation of the deceased going on. I remember how I'd had to stop myself from nodding when I read her textbook outpourings.

I put the file down on the table in front of me and let my eyes to drift around the staff room, with its filing cabinets, strewn back issues of journals and array of mugs on the draining board in the corner kitchenette. My tired eyes relaxed as I softened my focus; a rest from poring over handwriting that was getting increasingly hard to decipher as Fleur wrote more quickly, in time with her thoughts. I closed my eyes for a moment and opened them. I still couldn't totally ground myself in this room, here and now. A part of my mind remained in that previous time last year, when I was taking in Fleur's writing and at the same time stealing glances at her, observing that she no longer sat on the edge of her seat watching me, but had allowed herself to sit back and relax somewhat.

I picked up the document again and pressed on. Of course, my current reading of it was with the benefit of hindsight, of knowing the full story. I lingered over one of the passages:

We used to enjoy our holidays so much. We started to go to El Médano regularly, because Michael liked to go windsurfing there (it's a big centre for windsurfing). It's hardly a pretty place, but I grew to love it over the few years that we went there. There's no grass at all, the streets are narrow and higgly-piggly and it's usually wild and windswept (hence the windsurfing), but it was a clean wind that made you feel alive, invigorated. The beaches had dark grey volcanic sand, which took a bit of getting used to. What was really dramatic was Montaña Roja, a giant red peninsula sticking up out of the sea, all on its own amongst the greyness. If there was a day without wind we would gasp our way to the top (well, Michael didn't do much gasping) and take in the view over the sparkly coast on one side and up to Teide, the mountain in the middle of the island, on the other side. Then we would retrace our steps down the slopes, back to El Médano.

I didn't windsurf myself – not my thing at all – but I was perfectly happy spending my days walking around the streets and boardwalks or sitting in a sheltered place reading, and glancing up now and again to watch the colourful sails of the windsurfers soar over the surface of the sea, like gigantic butterflies. Viewed from the shore, they looked so graceful and elegant, although I knew from what Michael told me that you needed considerable skill and strength to handle one of them in those conditions of sea and wind. In fact, I learned a lot about windsurfing in my landlubber way.

Later in the afternoon, Michael would come back to our little apartment, glowing from the sun and wind, and full of stories of his exploits. Our balcony was right on the edge of the boardwalk and elevated a couple of storeys, so the view over the sea was amazing. We would laze around, hypnotised by the waves and watching the sunset, a glass of wine in our hand. I would have a fleece around my shoulders against the chill that could descend there in the evening.

It's funny, you wouldn't think I would be able to write about El Médano after what happened, but the place itself seems to be in a different, enchanted compartment in my mind. I don't suppose I could ever bear to go back there again now. Would I even want to?

I pored anew over these four paragraphs. A vividness and

fluency had infused her description of the little Spanish town; her writing conveyed for me the quirky charm of the place and its windsurfers. The detail of the text had inferred the link for her between Michael's untimely death and El Médano. Then, as if she had ventured too close for comfort, she had veered back to writing about their typical daily life at home. The prose became stilted, factual and slightly awkward again. Plenty of detail, but still skirting around the main issue. *'Client still reluctant to engage'* I had written in my notes.

'You've certainly written an interesting account of your life with Michael,' I had said after my brief read-through. 'I notice, though, that you haven't yet got to the part about when he died.'

Her one hand was stroking the end of the long plait of hair that draped over her shoulder. She said nothing.

I was as gentle as I could be. 'I know you've come to me to get some help in dealing with your grief. And I *can* help you. But first, Fleur, I need to know more about the circumstances of Michael's death before we can start addressing your healing process. We're nearly out of time today, but next week when we meet I'd like us to start talking about when Michael died. I know it will be painful for you. Write it down if that helps you. Could we do that, Fleur?'

At first I thought she was going to refuse, and that I had misjudged the timing. Then after a minute she said, so low that I could only just catch the words, 'I'll try.'

Chapter 4

'How are you today, Fleur?'

'I'm OK.'

A conventional enough opening exchange. On this day, our third session, there was a wariness, a tension, a slightly raised breathing rate accompanying her usual strained, haunted look. I noticed that she hadn't brought a sheaf of notes this time, and I commented on this.

'You said you wanted me to tell you about what happened to Michael. I tried to write it down, like I had been doing, but it wasn't working.' Her voice was jerky.

I sat back in my chair, crossed my legs, closed my notebook and put it down. 'Then just tell me in your own words. Let it come out in any way it wants to.'

She picked up the end of her plait and fingered it, in a way I was starting to recognise.

'I want to tell you everything. Even little things.'

I nodded. 'That's good. It's often the little things that are revealing, so include anything that comes into your mind. If it's OK with you, I'd like to record the session so that I can review it later, like I've been able to do with your written journal.'

She agreed. I set up the digital recorder and waited.

She fixed her gaze across the room, away from me, and started speaking in a neutral voice. 'It was three days before the end of our holiday. After a slow start that morning with only a slight breeze, by about eleven o'clock the wind had come in strong and steady, a perfect windsurfing day. Michael got ready to go down to the Centre where he hired the kit. He always brought his own harness with him on holiday, but he had to hire a board and sail. Usually he would come back to the apartment for lunch, in his wetsuit, and then go back in the afternoon. But today he was starting later, having waited for the wind to get up, so he said he wouldn't come back for lunch. This was also because the weather forecast – which was usually accurate about wind speed– said that the following two days were not going to be windy, so this was his last chance of the holiday for some good windsurfing. He kissed me on his way out, after he'd told me that he wouldn't be back at lunchtime. I was engrossed in my novel and so I didn't take too much notice. I never dreamed that this would be the last time I would see him.'

Her speech was mechanical, as if she were giving a statement, and I got the impression that she had rehearsed this in her head several times.

'I followed my general pattern for the morning. That was, I read my book, took a stroll along the boardwalk, enjoyed the sun and the bracing wind and had a coffee in my favourite place. Later I did something different. I picked out a bar on the boardwalk next to the beach and had lunch there. It seemed rather odd to me, that change of routine. We normally had all our meals together. Nevertheless, I quite enjoyed it. I could see the windsurfers and kitesurfers out to sea, speeding over the water. I could always spend ages looking at them, so colourful and graceful in their own way.

'After lunch I walked on to the town square, the plaza, which is right next to the beach. There's a little cluster of bars tucked into a corner there. I chose one and settled down to linger and watch the world go by. It was a Saturday, and as usual the town had come alive with day visitors from inland towns on the island. On a weekend the Spanish people could easily outnumber the holidaymakers if the weather was sunny, and the promenade gets thronged with everyone from strolling families with babies to elderly couples holding hands and everything inbetween. Also there were various buskers and jugglers doing their thing, giving the whole scene a bit of a raffish, benign, fiesta atmosphere. On the horizon the Red Mountain, Montaña Roja, reared up out of the sea. I should explain that this beautiful big hill has a graceful, pleasing profile that just seems to arise from nowhere and stand guard over the town. I think that El Médano is a special place, with an almost spiritual quality in its way, although I don't know quite what I mean by that.

'I can remember it very clearly, that afternoon sitting there in the sun with the flow of a busy Saturday going on around me. Looking back, everything seems emphasised, outlined, shimmering. I remember feeling connected with everything and everyone around me, but at the same time content to be alone in my own space. Was it really like that or am I just imagining it in hindsight? I don't know.

'Then a strange thing happened, and I know I'm not making this up. There is an iconic historic hotel, the Hotel Médano, which stands jutting out to sea next to the square. Part of it is actually built out over the water, on stilts. I was gazing up at the hotel with its white pristine rows of balconies when suddenly I thought, *if I were to come here on my own, I could stay there.* It just popped into my head unbidden. Why on earth would I want to come to El Médano on my own? All my holidays were with Michael. It was a surreal and slightly perplexing experience.

'After that I decided to move on. I thought I might as well go back to the apartment. On the way I lingered to listen to a young man playing a guitar. It sounded like flamenco to me, but I'm no expert. Passionate and Spanish sounding, anyway. He was very good; much too good to be playing in the street. I gave him a Euro and he smiled at me. It was about three-thirty by this time, and I pulled out my phone to check it. No message. Well, that was fine, I told myself. Michael said he was going to make the most of his last day. Although, surely he would have come ashore once, to get a drink or something? Usually he texted me when he did. Just a few words, such as: *Hi darling, come in to change my sail. Hope you're enjoying your day xx,* or *Just finished, I'll be back in about half an hour. Love you x.*

'I got back to the apartment and checked my phone again. Four o'clock and no word. Then four-thirty and still nothing. To tell the truth, and I feel ashamed to say it now, I was slightly annoyed. I knew it was going to be his last day windsurfing, but you'd think he would have had time to send a text. When it got to nearly five o'clock – which was when all the hired equipment was supposed to be back in the Centre – I decided to walk down and meet him. I rarely did that, because he would be laughing and joking with the others and talking about their sport. I could never join in, and it made me feel awkward.

'At the Centre sails and boards were being washed down with hoses and put on racks. When I didn't see Michael I asked one of the boys behind the desk if he knew where he was. He said he hadn't seen him. He called across and asked the other staff. Nobody knew of him coming back in during the afternoon, his locker still contained his clothes and no-one had seen him. No-one had seen him.

'Then the nightmare started. They said they would organise a search. The manager of the centre, Hans, went with me to the Lifeguard Station and they sent out the lifeboat and a jetski to look for him. The head of the lifeguards explained to me, in broken English because I speak hardly any Spanish, that they would search on the water now but they couldn't send the helicopter out because it would be starting to get dark before long. I stood there, helpless and numb. Eventually someone got me a chair and a blanket. The lifeguards and the police – they had arrived by then – milled around and I could hear them speaking into their radios, although it was all unintelligible gabbling to me because of course it was in Spanish.

'It's hard to explain how I felt. The closest I can get is that it was like I was acting a part in a play, except that I didn't know my lines. None of this was really happening; none of it was real at all. How could it be? I don't know how much time had gone by when a policeman came up and managed to make me understand that I needed to fill in a Missing Person's Report. I told him I would go tomorrow morning. He shook his head. "No," he said. "Now. You go now".

'I don't know quite what I would have done if Hans hadn't stepped forward then and offered to take me. You see, the Police

31

Station was in Granadilla, a town up in the hills about half an hour away by car, in the hinterland behind El Médano. We drove up the narrow twisting mountain roads. Hans was anxious to reassure me that the helicopter would find Michael the next day and that he would be able to cling onto his board until then. But what if he's injured, I said? What if he's weak and exhausted? Hans reached over and squeezed my hand. "Pray," he said.

'We waited for what seemed like ages in the grimy Police Station with its plastic chairs and enclosed smell. Eventually we were taken to a little room with harsh lighting where this weary looking officer chatted quite normally with Hans before he turned to his computer and logged onto the form. All in a day's work for him, I suppose. I don't know how many languages Hans speaks, but he's certainly fluent in Spanish and English. The questions were all what you might expect, when did you last see your husband etc, all translated by Hans. I gave my answers as best I could… oh yes, and at some stage someone brought me a bottle of water and a sandwich.

'It was very late when Hans drove me back down the dark mountain roads. The lights of the coastal towns twinkling below us, sort of mirroring the stars above us. I felt like I was suspended there with them, floating outside of my body. He praised how calm I was. When I look back, I know it wasn't really calm, it was shock. I was in shock.

'The apartment was empty and still, like it was hardly breathing. I noticed some of Michael's clothes were on the floor where he'd left them. I picked up a T-shirt and buried my face in it, trying to inhale his smell. I wandered about. I didn't know what to do with myself. We had a bottle of licor 43 in the apartment, that's the local Spanish drink. We were going to take it home as a present for someone, but instead I unscrewed it and drank it straight from the bottle. It was sweet and pretty revolting, but I drank it down anyway.'

During her monologue Fleur had barely moved – neither had I, for that matter. Now she stirred and said, 'Could I possibly

32

have a glass of water?'

I poured her one from the fresh carafe on the side table and asked if she wanted to take a break. She shook her head, her eyes steady over the rim of the glass. I was keeping a close watch on her. She seemed composed enough, and her determination today to recite what had happened to Michael didn't seem to be overtaxing her.

She picked straight up where she'd left off, fixing her gaze once more across the room. 'I lay in bed in the dark. You would think, wouldn't you, that I would have been screaming, hysterical, but I wasn't. The same thought patterns chased each other round and round in my head. First, I sent out my love and thoughts to Michael, there in the cold, dark water, clinging to his board. Hold on, I whispered. Just hold on a few hours longer, my darling. They'll come and find you in the morning. Then I thought, but what happened? Why did nobody see him? Why did the Lifeboat not find him? *Where is he?* And then I thought, there must have been a freak wave or something and he's dead. He's already dead. He must be… and then I'd go back to the beginning again, pleading with him to stay strong.

'Hans said about praying. Now, I'm not religious. I don't even think I believe in God. But I certainly prayed that night. God please keep my Michael safe, God please let him be alright, God I will do *anything…*

'Eventually I must have fallen asleep because I woke up and it was daylight and I could hear the noise of a helicopter overhead. Just for a minute, I thought it had all been a dream – the Lifeboat, the police, the dark journey inland, filling in the report - then the reality came crashing in. I stumbled out of bed and went to the window in time to see the rescue helicopter heading out over the sea. They're out early, I thought. They're going to find him!

'My initial optimism waned as much of the day passed with neither the head lifeguard nor Hans getting in touch with me. The lifeguards had no news, although they were searching all the time, and Hans tried his best to keep my spirits up. I started phoning or messaging various people – family, a few close friends. Then the calls and messages started coming back, full of disbelief and horror. It's not what you expect to get on a peaceful Sunday morning, is it? *Hi, this just to say that Michael is missing at sea, feared drowned...* But there was so much love and support in the replies. I decided not to get in touch with Michael's parents at this stage, until I knew more. They live in Australia, and after all, what could they do?

'Mid-afternoon and there was still nothing. The phone rang and it was my older brother, Hugo. I had phoned him in the morning – in fact he was the first person I phoned – and I'd talked to him again around midday. To my absolute surprise he said he was at the airport, in the Departure Lounge ready to board the plane to Tenerife, and he'd be with me by early evening. He didn't say, "Shall I come to Tenerife? Do you need me?" He just came. He knew if he'd said that, I would have said no, I can manage. After all, he has a young family and a responsible job. I felt absurdly lifted and hopeful, knowing that he was coming. Hugo would sort it all out, Hugo would make it all alright, just like when I was six and he was fourteen. He'd always been a lovely big brother to me and he got on really well with Michael.

'It's when I saw him get out of the taxi outside the apartment that I broke down. I stood and howled, his arms round me, holding me up. Then we went inside and he had me tell him everything, in detail. He asked if he could go and meet the head lifeguard and Hans. He always was one who could take charge of a situation, was Hugo... That evening he said we should go out and get something to eat, even though I didn't feel like it. We talked. Not about what was happening, but he led me into talking about our childhood, holidays, pets, anecdotes. You know, silly stuff. Oh, and we phoned Mum and Dad, and talked to them together. They were reassured to know that Hugo was with me.

'I didn't sleep too badly that night, strangely enough. I was probably exhausted. Then the next day the nightmare continued. We watched the helicopter go out over the sea again. Hugo said gently that they wouldn't be able to keep up the search much longer. It had been two nights now and well… I should prepare myself.

'It was late morning when the call came through from the police. A fishing boat off the coast of Los Cristianos – that's a port some miles away - had found a male body in the water. They arranged for me to meet with some police officials that afternoon, in a quiet little garden in the other hotel in El Médano.

'Do you know, I remember exactly how that garden looked. The way the sunlight came through the trees, the white tables and chairs, the exotic greenery, which was unusual for El Médano… Hugo and I waited, not knowing exactly what to expect. This was it, I knew that much. "It's not every day that they find a man's body in the water," Hugo said, holding my hand. "It's too much to hope for that it's not Michael".

'The policemen – detectives, I suppose – were in smart plain clothes, trousers and short-sleeved shirts. They were both tall and broad and wore sunglasses. They didn't smile. After introducing themselves in good English, they asked to see my passport and Michael's, and briefly went over again everything that had happened. Then, one of them drew a plastic bag out of his briefcase, took a watch out of it and put it on the table. He asked if I had seen it before. Of course I'd seen it before. It was nothing special, just a standard sports watch, a divers' watch, in fact. I remember being surprised that it was still going. I asked if I could pick it up. The metal was hard between my fingers. Once again, I felt as if I was outside of my body, looking down on this curious scene of me signing the Spanish form to confirm that I identified the watch as Michael's. Signing Michael away… And that was it. That's all it took. They both said that they were very sorry for my loss. It occurred to me to be surprised that they knew that English expression, "very sorry for your loss". The words went round and round in my head while Hugo walked back with me to the apartment. Very sorry for your loss.

'Hugo told me that it was better that they had actually found his body than not. That would have caused very messy complications for you, he said. Ever the solicitor, our Hugo. Perhaps I hadn't mentioned that he's a solicitor? You can't imagine how glad I was that he was with me. He was an absolute rock. He dealt with all the relevant people: the British Consul, my holiday insurers, various people at home and the undertakers when they came. Oh yes, and Hans acted as interpreter again. So kind of him, too. I answered questions when they were put to me, but I was just… just inert. I couldn't take it in. *Very sorry for your loss.*'

I watched Fleur carefully. Her gaze was unfocussed and she was very still. She was reliving the same automaton-like state that she had so vividly described. It popped into my head to wonder if this was a sort of self-hypnosis, a coping strategy. Kai would know. 'Fleur, thank you for telling me how Michael died. I can see what an effort it was for you, so perhaps we should stop there. You've been incredibly brave today.'

She frowned and shook her head, turning to face me. For the first time today she seemed agitated.

'But I haven't got to the important part. I need to tell you now.'

'What is the important part, Fleur?'

'You see, I didn't go to see his body. They asked me if I wanted to, but I couldn't face it. I said no. He would have looked terrible, having been in the water all that time. I was a coward.' She took the end of her plait and stroked it rapidly as if it were a small pet.

'I think that was a good decision that you made. There was nothing to be gained by seeing his body, and it would have been very upsetting for you.'

'But that's not all. They couldn't say when the funeral would be, because there would need to be a post-mortem. It could be days and days.' Her voice rose. 'All I wanted to do was go home.

36

My flight home after the end of the holiday was booked for the next day. The Consul said I was free to go, so I flew home. Hugo took me home. I didn't go to Michael's funeral. I didn't go to my own husband's funeral.'

She was very upset now and I strove to calm her down. 'That's perfectly understandable, under the circumstances. I can see -'

She shook her head violently. 'No, no, that's not it. I didn't see *him*. All I saw was his watch. I didn't see his body. How do I really know it was him? *What if he's not really dead?*'

Chapter 5

'Reiki? Even perhaps aromatherapy? I ask you! We'll be having a nail bar in the practice next!'

Cora, to give her her due, took the flak while I let rip all the frustration that had built up since I'd sat through a hastily called extra team meeting that morning and Neville had made his cool announcement of his vision for the practice.

'Hypnotherapy, OK. I've more or less come around to that now, having talked to Kai and learned a bit about its merits. But reiki… that can't have any place alongside proper psychotherapy and counselling. And aromatherapy is just perfumes and pampering, surely?' Cora didn't reply. Her expression was mainly hidden behind a pair of enormous sunglasses. 'Well it is, isn't it?' I prompted.

'I don't have any experience of reiki therapy myself, but I have friends who swear by it. And I love having an aromatherapy massage, although I admit I don't think of it as therapy.'

'It's pseudoscience, fringe medicine, New Age mumbo-jumbo.'

'If it helps people, surely it's worth considering.' I sensed her raised eyebrows behind the sunglasses.

'You're missing the point! Those sorts of things will only discredit the serious counselling work of the practice.' She wasn't saying what I wanted to hear. Surely your girlfriend is supposed to support you, to offer sympathy and understanding, to make soothing murmuring sounds… like Lisa used to, in fact. Whoa! I took a deep breath and hauled myself back from both those ridiculous trains of thought, born of my frustration with the morning's meeting.

When Neville had unveiled his grand plans there had been a bewildered silence around the table, and puzzled glances exchanged between Emma (recently back from her sickness), Stacey and the others. It was only me who voiced concerns –

quite calmly, to give me credit - but Neville with his urbane smile trotted out a lot of bullshit about 'diversification' and 'enhancing the clients' experience' and exhorted us to see the practice in terms of its broadest aspiration, a one-stop-shop for mental wellbeing, as set out in his vision. It made me want to puke.

Cora sucked up the last of her cocktail through a straw. 'I'm going to get another drink. Same again?' I hardly listened to her reply.

The wait at the bar did me good. I felt my pulse beat slow as I did my little trick to ground myself in the here-and-now rather than back in time where my thoughts were swirling. What you do is simply look around your surroundings and deliberately choose and name five things you can see. The open door to the terrace, a beer mat on the counter, the sign to the toilets, a worn patch on the carpet, a girl in a short red dress with her legs crossed. There. An old calming device that I use with clients now and again. Simple, but it works if you allow it to.

I took the drinks back to our table on the terrace. A riverside pub, complete with ducks, swans and boats, had to be the perfect spot on a bright early evening after work. 'Sorry,' I said. 'I didn't mean to take it out on you. I got pretty worked up this morning, then I was busy all afternoon, so I was letting off steam.'

She nodded, which presumably was an acknowledgement of my apology. 'Would there be any mileage in getting feedback from your clients? Do they fill in any sort of appraisal form at the end of their sessions? Perhaps you could add some questions on other therapies or treatments that they would like to see offered. And it gives you something constructive to offer Neville, rather than simply disagreeing with him and challenging him for the alpha male slot.'

I spluttered over my lager. 'Me? I've never seen myself as an alpha male! And since when have you been the psychologist here?'

She shrugged, irritatingly cool and feminine. 'Just a thought.' She turned to look at two ducks squawking noisily over a piece of bread. Alpha males, I dare say.

Actually, when I thought about it, she could have a point. I could get the rest of the staff onside about these extra questions on the exit survey. In fact, it was a neat move. Provided the clients came back with saying that they didn't want any of this New Age stuff, of course. And I could live with my woman seeing me as the alpha type.

'That's a good idea. I'll sound out the others and we could present it at the next meeting. Thank you, darling.'

She smiled somewhat smugly, as well she might. 'And now, do you want to hear about my day? I have some news.'

I was at once filled with compunction at having got in first and hogged the conversational stage. She took off her sunglasses and I could see her eyes twinkling. 'You know how I've been angling to get my own exhibition for ages? Well, I think I've got a backer and it could happen soon. Before the autumn, anyway.' She went on to tell me the details, her voice full of subdued excitement.

I was genuinely pleased for her. She worked away at a job she didn't like that much, hoping that her own work would get more attention. 'That's brilliant! And here was me ranting on while you patiently waited to tell me that.' We went on to brainstorm potential venues and which pieces she might include. Not that I was much help with either, but I provided a willing sounding board.

When she went to the Ladies' room, I did my habitual thing – a bad thing, really - of pulling my phone out to check my messages. There was one from Lisa: '*There's a last minute cancellation on a school trip to France and N would really like to go. Sorry to drop this on you but we need to decide as soon as. What do you think? X*'. I could make a good shot at reading between the lines. School trips were not usually what Nathan considered cool, so him suddenly wanting to go on this one now probably implied some reason other than an interest in foreign culture and broadening his horizons. Also I knew that I would be required to stump up for this trip. That was fine. Lisa didn't earn much, and it would help to assuage my guilt, never entirely quashed, for leaving her. You didn't need to be a shrink to work that one out. Hundreds of dads up and down the country would feel the same thing. Well, it would depend on just how much this jaunt was going to cost and what exactly were Nathan's motives.

I had started to reply when I saw Cora coming back – I still couldn't stop myself doing a double-take about the asymmetric hair, not to mention the purple colouring – so I curtailed the message with *I'll phone you either later or tomorrow X.*

'Anything important?' she asked conversationally as I hastily pressed 'send'.

'Nothing that can't wait.' I wasn't about to rock any boats there, particularly since I hadn't yet plucked up the courage to show Joe's picture to Cora. Well, maybe now would be as good a time as any, what with her being in a good mood about her exhibition.

'Can I show you something? I'd like your professional opinion.' I pulled the picture out of my bag, where it was starting to get a bit battered, passed it to her and waited while she scrutinised it.

'Did you do this?'

I threw my head back and guffawed. 'You must be joking! I haven't got an artistic bone in my body. No, Joe did it. He didn't copy it, he just made it up out of his head. I think it's brilliant, but what do you think?'

She handed it back to me. 'It's a nice little sketch.'

'A nice little... Joe's only six, and he has learning difficulties, if you remember.'

'What does his teacher say?'

I had to admit that I didn't know, and I asked her if she thought he had talent and did she have any ideas about how to take this forward. This was her field, after all.

She sighed and spread her hands out. 'Simon, I really don't know anything about autistic children. I don't know anything about children, full stop.' *And why are you bothering, he's not your son,* was the bit she didn't say.

I should have known better. I really should have known better. I had thought it wouldn't be too much to expect that her interest would be aroused, and that she would overcome her jealousy of my ex-wife and kids enough to at least give me a few pointers. How could I explain to her that I felt partly responsible for Joe's birth? If I hadn't left Lisa, she wouldn't have gone on that holiday and got herself pregnant with Joe. And yes, if that's not fucked up thinking, I don't know what is.

*

'That was a demanding session for you last week, Fleur. You did very well.'

She looked pale and tired, but I thought rather less anguished this time. She'd got to the heart of what was preventing her grief from resolving itself. I needed to be gentle easing her back into the revelations from last week, so I first asked her how her week had been, and if she had done anything interesting.

'I went to stay with Hugo and his family for the weekend.'

'Ah, your brother. How did that go?'

'It was good. The children are always a distraction, and I get on well with my sister-in-law.' After continuing in a neutral voice to tell me about a trip to a stately home and a picnic, she said that Hugo had asked how the counselling sessions were going. In fact, she told me, it was he who had suggested that she should see someone about her grief. 'He doesn't know about the other thing, though,' she added.

'What do you mean by "the other thing", Fleur?'

I had to wait for her answer. 'That it's possible the body they found wasn't Michael.'

'Since Hugo was with you and supported you during that time in El Médano, it makes me wonder why you didn't share your thoughts with him.' I had chosen my words carefully so as not to refer to Michael's death.

She took hold of the end of her plait and curled her fingers around it. Her shoulders were hunched. 'In the beginning I just let everything happen around me. It's only in these last few weeks that I've had this feeling, this nagging doubt. You see, I didn't see the body. I didn't see Michael. So how can I be sure? I haven't told Hugo because he thinks I'm getting over it and I don't want to worry him.'

'Yes, I can see that you wouldn't want to trouble him. I suggest, Fleur, that today you carry on telling me the story. You had got to where you were coming home from El Médano. Tell me what else happened.'

'Alright.' She settled back in her chair and was silent for a couple of minutes. I stilled my body and mind and waited.

'I can't quite remember where I'd got to. The undertakers came to the apartment in El Médano... I'm not sure if I told you that? No? Well, Hugo handled it all really. And Hans came again to be our translator. Hugo was ages on the phone with my insurance company. I know there was some wrangling about payment for the funeral and cremation. I just sat there and let them get on with it. It seemed so bizarre, these people whom I didn't know in the apartment, and this strange translated conversation. I felt as if I were outside looking in on everybody, like a scene in a play. Oh, and that's when they asked me if I wanted to see the body. I remember looking to Hugo for guidance, as I did with every question they asked, and he said I didn't have to see it if I didn't want to, and that it would probably be very traumatic. So I agreed not to. How I wish now that I had been brave enough...

'The British Consul lady phoned us again later on. She had been very nice all along, guiding us through what we had to do. I asked her when we would be free to go home, and she said if the funeral was all sorted out – the disposal of the body, she said – we could go any time we liked and all the paperwork would be posted on to us in due course. All I took in from what she said was that I could leave this place, which was now like a nightmare, and go home. Home. Everything would be better at home.

'So Hugo got a seat on the return flight with me and took me home. Mum and Dad were there waiting for us and we had to tell the whole story over again. I was surprised at how composed I felt. Well, that lasted until just after they had all left. My parents had wanted to stay, but I insisted that I wanted to be on my own. I went upstairs to the bedroom. I opened Michael's wardrobe and there were all his clothes. And it hit me like an express train. He was not coming back. Ever. Far from being better at home, now it was all suddenly real. I phoned Mum and Dad in their car – they'd have been gone less than half an hour – and cried hysterically down the phone. They turned straight round and came back, bless them.'

She put her face in her hands, and I was just about able to make out that she was saying she didn't want to think about that day anymore. I could see the light, downy hairs on her forearms, her short nails, and the neat gold wristwatch on her left wrist. A diamond glinted in her engagement ring. I was just about to intervene when she raised her head again and said, 'I can't really recall much about the next few weeks. I seemed to just go through the motions of the days on autopilot. I cried a lot. It was impossible to believe what had happened. There were cards, emails, callers, flowers, a small piece in the local paper… My employers were brilliant. They arranged for me to have time off and a phased return when I was ready. Everyone was shocked.'

She was less composed and focussed than during the previous session, and I didn't want to overtax her. 'I know this is difficult for you, Fleur, but I'm sure you'll understand that in order for me to help you, I need to get straight in my mind the more formal things associated with why you've come to me for help. I'd like to guide you with a few questions, if I may. Or would you like to take a short break?' When she said she was OK to continue, I referred back to the paperwork that she had mentioned earlier, and asked if that included a Death Certificate. Somewhat to my surprise she reached into her bag and pulled out a plastic file. I hadn't expected her to be that organised. She passed me three documents and told me that they were the Cause of Death with permission to incinerate the body, the Death Certificate and a more lengthy report on the autopsy. She told me that the first two documents arrived within a few days of her returning home whereas the autopsy report took a few weeks.

I gazed at the pages in my hands, the first two bearing official seals in blue ink. Even though I spoke no Spanish, it wasn't hard to work out that *Certificacion del Acta de Defuncion* was Michael's Death Certificate. *Defuncion*... to stop functioning, presumably. What an apt description of death. I looked over the contents of the documents, but the words were a meaningless jumble to me. I found this opacity strangely disconcerting. It undermined my control of the situation. 'Where does it state the cause of death?' I asked.

She pointed to where it said, *Causa de la muerte: anoxia encefalica.* 'Lack of oxygen to the brain. And on the line above it means "mechanical asphyxiation by submersion".' Her voice was toneless.

It was frustrating, this not being able to understand most of the words in front of me. I pointed to the line she'd just referred to. 'What's this other thing... *cardiopatia isquemica*?' I stumbled over the pronunciation.

'It means restriction of the blood supply to his heart.'

'Let me make sure I understand this. They discovered during the post-mortem that Michael had had a heart attack before he died? And that would be why he fell off the board and drowned?'

She nodded. Tears were filling her eyes now. 'How could anyone think that Michael had a weak heart? He was so active.'

'I'm not medically trained, but I understand that this sort of weakness can go undetected in the body for a long while.'

She didn't answer. I sat with her for couple of minutes, giving her space in the cocooning silence. Then I said, 'Fleur,

45

would you mind if I take a photocopy of these documents to keep in your file? I'll only be a couple of minutes.'

When she agreed I took the papers out to Lucy in reception. She was intent on her computer screen, the fan on her desk humming gently as it turned. Her hair lifted slightly off her neck with each rotation. 'Lucy, can you run off a quick copy of these, please?' I asked. She complied with a cheery smile, as always. There was a quick widening of her eyes when she saw the texts were not in English, but she made no comment, well trained as she was. When she got up her skirt was stuck to her legs and bottom, and she gave a quick tweak to release it. I listened to the clicks and whirrs of the photocopier as they accompanied the desk fan.

*

I put Fleur's file down on the desk with a sigh, shut my eyes and stretched my back. What a bloody great wadge of notes I had generated last year! The photocopies of the certificates were in front of me, along with my scribbled pages. I can't really remember those details of Lucy making the photocopies; of course I can't. My mind was just filling in the blanks with something that fits, as minds do, given half a chance. That's the trouble with memory. I do remember the whole thing about the fan and Lucy getting up from her desk – I think – but it might well have been another day.

So even though there's a shedfull of notes for me to wade through, they are a definitive record of my sessions with Fleur, rather than any reliance on memory – that's the whole point of keeping them, after all. I read again my summary for the fourth session: *FB brought evidence of MB's death, viz. three official documents in Spanish. A heart attack/defect provides a credible reason for subsequent death by drowning. FB still not able to accept the reality of the death, Preliminary steps taken in the session to address her persistent guilt about not viewing the body or attending the funeral.*

I had recorded in my notes from the session that Fleur had

asked me outright if I believed that Michael could still be alive. Neatly, she gave me the opportunity I needed to plant the first seeds.

'Fleur, you went through all the formalities with the Spanish authorities. Identification-'

'But I didn't identify *him*. It was just his watch.'

I chose my words carefully. 'That was enough to satisfy the detectives, and they must have known their business. Neither the Spanish authorities nor the British Consulate would have allowed the death to be recorded if they weren't absolutely positive that this was Michael Bentley. And presumably the Coroner here in the UK was satisfied?' She nodded, her face averted. 'Supposing for a minute, just supposing, that the body had been someone else's. He would surely have been reported missing. And if it wasn't Michael who was cremated, where is Michael now?' I spoke as gently as I could.

'But I didn't actually see him,' she whispered. 'And I didn't go to his funeral.'

'I know you didn't, and that you regret that.' I took care to validate her feelings. 'Nevertheless, I would like you to consider this: you are punishing yourself when you don't need to. You have nothing, nothing at all, to feel remorseful or guilty about. It wasn't even a mistake, it was a wise choice. What's happening is that your mind is clutching at past events rather than accepting the truth, which is that Michael did die in a drowning accident. You've got yourself stuck in that place and it's impeding your grief and giving you a lot of extra suffering.' I gave her chance to absorb my quiet words and then I added, 'I know this is a lot to take in, and you don't have to deal with it all at once. Next week we can start looking at ways to help you move on and heal.'

Her hand sought the end of her plait in her usual comfort strategy. I looked at the heavy rope of hair and it came to me suddenly to wonder what it would be like loose, that abundant waterfall. How would it look if Fleur were lying on a bed and her hair was spread out and overflowed the pillows? Sometimes memories dilute over time, and you've distorted them or slotted them in the wrong place. Other times, memories are piercing certainties.

Chapter 6

'So you're not keen on having an aromatherapist in the practice either?' said Kai. 'I didn't think you would be. It could be a good idea of yours to have a few leading questions at the end of the clients' exit questionnaire about what they would like to see on offer. I don't think Neville's going to like it, though.'

'Neville's a twat.' When you're halfway down your second pint you don't feel like mincing your words.

'Maybe so. But he's a twat who's given me a job. I'm still the new boy so I have to toe the line a bit more than you. Anyway, enough of that. Guess what I've done?'

I eyed him for clues. He was grinning, full of suppressed excitement. 'Got a tattoo on your backside?'

'Nope.'

'I give up. What have you done?' I was more than ready to be distracted from the politics in the practice.

'I've decided to give Tinder a go.'

I raised my eyebrows. 'Wouldn't it be a good idea to wait until you're divorced before you start dating again?' Kai and I were on plain speaking terms now. A relief from the circumlocutions with clients at work.

Kai leant back and spread his arms along the back of his bench seat. The 'Legend' T-shirt seemed to be one of his favourites. I didn't think it got washed very often, but I wasn't about to say anything. 'Maybe. But I'm fed up with evenings on my own. Didn't think it would hurt to dip my toe in the water. See what's out there, you know. Haven't you ever dabbled?'

To be honest, I hadn't. That didn't stop Kai giving me chapter and verse about his forays so far (I think her profile picture must have been taken twenty years ago… shit, I've never seen a woman drink so much… all she could talk about was her ex…). I was pretty sure he'd dipped more than his toe, but I didn't especially want the lowdown on that too. Anyway, I was happy this evening to sit back and be entertained. It was as good a way as any to flush out the day, and I couldn't be bothered to keep up my end of the conversation with news of my world – Nathan's sudden trip to France and the conversations that Cora and I kept not having about our holiday.

I mulled the evening over on my way home later. No, I'd never used a dating app. I'd met Cora in a wine bar, and other girlfriends in similar places. Lisa and I had first seen each other around the campus when we were both at university. When she's not looking frazzled like she often is nowadays, she still has that open prettiness that attracted me fifteen years ago. A sort of a rotund wholesomeness. She had looked like that yesterday when I called round to sort out this school trip business.

Nathan and I had gone for a walk to the local park. It wasn't bad, as parks went, and certainly well used. We strolled over the grass, which was getting a bit threadbare here and there. We tacitly avoided the playground in the one corner, gravitating instead to quieter places under the trees. I realised that Nathan was as tall as me now, because when we turned slightly to say something to each other, we met eye to eye. First of all we went through the usual general chat, including my gentle catechism on what was going on in his life. I was quietly amused that he was more forthcoming than usual about his school work and what he was getting up to with his mates. It was clear he knew that best behaviour was called for – he'd probably been briefed by his Mum. I turned the conversation round to the French trip. He told me that it was for six days, setting off next week. They were going via the Channel Tunnel and staying in cheap hotels. I forget now the places he said they would be visiting, but Paris was the big climax. He assured me earnestly, upon my asking, that it would be brilliant for his French listening and speaking skills. I asked him if any of his friends were going, and he reeled off a short list, adding as if as an afterthought, that someone called Michelle was going. His eyes slid away from me and his neck coloured a dull red. Aha. There we had it.

I couldn't resist stringing him along a bit. Michelle was 'just some girl' he mumbled. I said solemnly that she had the right name for a visit to France. Or was she actually French? His flush deepened as he replied. Oh Nathan, son. I felt a father's relief that at fourteen his hormones were sending him timely messages, mixed with trepidation about the pitfalls of his forthcoming journey into manhood.

So I put him out of his misery and told him I'd pay for him to go, adding the corollary that he had to behave himself and be careful. How much of the last bit he heard, I don't know. He was too busy thumping my arm and whooping.

Back at the house he responded to Lisa's enquiring look with a big grin which she answered with a beaming smile and a thumbs up. This silent pantomime was because Nathan had warned me on the way back to the house that Mum didn't want Joe getting wind of anything yet in case it triggered one of his anxiety attacks. Changes to his daily routine wasn't something he handled well. Apparently he had just about accepted the idea of the holiday they were going on soon so it was thought best to keep it quiet until the last minute if Nathan was going away. To be fair, Nathan was very good with Joe on the whole.

Joe was sitting at the table scribbling when I went in. I sat down with him and asked to see what he was doing, but I didn't get much response. 'Remember that picture you drew for me? The one of the city? I've got it up on the wall in my kitchen.'

'It came out of my head,' he said, without taking his eyes away from what he was doing.

'I know. And it's brilliant. How about a high five?'

But it wasn't a high five day and I knew I shouldn't push it. Lisa came bustling in. She had her curling tong thingy in her hand and was giving the finishing touches to her hair. I say finishing touches because her hair was looking particularly nice already, I thought. Glossy and wavy. 'Sorry to rush around,' she said, 'but I'm going out soon. Mum's coming over to sit with Joe. You can stay longer if you like, though.'

We both knew what my response to that would be. I said my goodbyes to the boys and she saw me out. On the front step she put her hand on my arm and reached up to kiss me on the cheek. 'Thank you, Simon. I mean it. That was very generous.' She stroked my cheek with her finger and it took me a minute to realise that she was wiping the lipstick off.

'You're welcome. By the way, do you know there's a girl that Nathan fancies going on this trip?'

Her eyes widened. '*What*? He never said anything to me!'

'Well, he's hardly likely to tell his mum, is he? Look, I don't think we should overreact... he is nearly fifteen, after all. It's about time he took an active interest.'

Lisa looked doubtful. 'Have you had a talk with him yet? You know.'

'A talk? You mean birds and bees stuff? Surely nobody does that nowadays. I thought they picked it all up off the internet and from school.'

'God, no! If you just rely on that he'll pick up all sorts of distorted notions about what's normal. Don't you get any of this in your job?'

Frankly, no, because I didn't work with children. But I realised she probably had a point. 'But there won't be any chance to see him again before he goes away,' I said. 'I wouldn't worry, though. He's a sensible lad.'

'Like we were, you mean? Like I was when I got pregnant with Joe?'

Since she was obviously concerned about it, I agreed to WhatsApp him and be a bit more specific about the do's and don'ts. To change the subject, I said, 'You're looking really nice this evening.' She was, too. Her face seemed all sparkly and she was wearing a colourful swishy dress that accentuated her curves. I rarely saw her in make-up, a dress and high heels nowadays. 'Going somewhere nice?'

'It's a date,' she said. 'We're going for a meal.'

'Oh. Oh, I see. Been seeing him long?'

'This is our second date.'

The awkward pause was prevented from becoming even more so by an angry yell emanating from the house. Joe kicking off. 'Now what?' she said. 'I've got to go, but thanks again.' I stared at the front door, still ajar, and heard the bellowing subside after Lisa said something. I turned back to the street just in time to see the approach of Lisa's mum in her car. Time to go.

*

I was now coming up to reading the fifth out of a total of seven sessions that I had had with Fleur last year. The pile of notes in front of me, on the left-hand side of the desk, represented those that I had read. This pile was now considerably bigger than that on the right-hand side, which was the notes that I had yet to work through. It was a pity I couldn't have taken the file out of the office to read at home; I'd have read late into the night and finished them in one go. As it was, I was squeezing the reading into spaces in my already quite busy schedule during office hours.

My appointment with Fleur was still a few days away, but my monthly supervision was – perhaps fortuitously – coming up before that and I wanted to have it all refreshed in my head before then.

So I settled back to read session five. Ah yes, my notes brought it all back. I'm glad that I had got into methodical note-taking habits early on in my career. Fleur had come in looking vaguely harassed, I thought, rather different to her usual anguished demeanour. She was, as ever, dressed very femininely in a long gypsy-type skirt and a loose white blouse. I remember that outfit distinctly. I asked how she was. She responded automatically that she was OK. I followed up my opener by asking how her week had been.

'Actually, I had something really unexpected happen, the day after we met last time,' she burst out. I continued with my encouraging silence. 'It was to do with my holiday insurance. Hugo had had all the dealings with them about paying for the funeral and all that. Then a few weeks after I came home they contacted me and asked, was I putting a claim in for accidental death? I hadn't given it a thought, but I reasoned I might as well. I got together notarised copies of everything they asked for and sent them off with the form that I'd filled in. They said it would take a time to process, and I more or less forgot about it. Then this week, look what arrived.' She thrust a cheque at me.

'Fifty thousand pounds?' It was a stupid thing to say, since the cheque clearly was for that amount. But I felt wrongfooted; I wasn't sure where she was coming from, and what response she expected from me.

'Yes. Is that how much his life was worth? I never wanted to be *paid* for him to die. It's, like, blood money. I've already had our mortgage paid off under the life insurance, and now this…' She was breathing quite heavily now in her agitation.

I never wanted to be paid for him to die… I picked up on that. This time my silence was because I was considering the best response to take us forward.

She held the cheque carefully by its corners with two hands, as if it were contaminated, and frowned at it. 'As you can see, I haven't been able to bring myself to cash it yet.' She dropped it onto her lap with a huge sigh and looked directly at me. 'This means he really is dead, doesn't it?'

So that was it. 'He always *was* really dead, Fleur. But yes, I can see what you mean. No company would pay out that amount of money unless they were sure that the claim was genuine.'

She thought for a moment, noticeably struggling with something. 'I haven't mentioned this before, but I keep thinking… I know it can't…' she trailed off.

I said, 'You can say it, whatever it is. You're safe here.'

She took a deep breath and said, 'I think I've seen him. I think I've seen Michael.'

So, grief-induced hallucinations of the deceased. Classic.

'It will be somewhere busy, like a street. He had this hat that he used to wear a lot, it's a lightish coloured trilby with a dark band around it. A couple of weeks ago I glimpsed a man in a crowd ahead of me wearing a hat like that and I thought, "It's Michael! He's come back!" I struggled to get through the people, but he'd gone. I couldn't find him. I searched around, and I got quite upset.'

'Have you ever seen someone you thought was Michael, then got closer and discovered that it was just someone who looked a bit like him?'

She nodded. 'Several times. And that's horrible. For just a couple of minutes my heart leaps...'

'Do you see or hear him in your house?'

'Well, once I thought I heard him in the night. And I think I hear him putting his key in the lock.' She took a gulp from the glass of water by her side. 'Do you think I'm going mad?'

'Absolutely not. Hallucinations, that is thinking you see or hear the deceased loved one, are not uncommon in grief, especially after a traumatic death like Michael's. Most usually this happens in the home. We think bereavement-related hallucinations represent a compensatory effort to cope with the drastic sense of loss, as if the perception has yet to catch up with the knowledge of the beloved's passing.' I realised from her blankness that I'd gone too much into textbook mode. 'You could say it's nature's way of easing you gently into your adjusted life. Sometimes it can be rather scary, but I can assure you it's a normal phenomenon. You're definitely not going crazy.'

She looked at me doubtfully so I continued, 'As for you thinking you see Michael in the street, that comes down to the belief that you were holding on to about him still being alive. And it sounds like it was a very distinctive hat that Michael often wore. When you saw a similar hat it would have served as a potent symbol of him. Now that you are accepting the truth of Michael's death, you can let go of these reactions, Fleur. A person you see in the street who looks a bit like your husband is simply just that.' She didn't answer, and I was aware she needed processing time on this and I didn't want to lead her faster than she was able to go. So after a minute I changed tack and asked her if there had been any sort of commemorative event for Michael, to celebrate his life.

'Oh, haven't I told you about that? Yes, there was a full memorial service in our church. It wasn't until a month after... after I came back from Tenerife, because I wanted to have received his ashes first. The ashes... the whole business about ashes seems bizarre to me. Some friends who went on holiday to Tenerife brought them back for me. They were in a big plastic tub like... oh, I don't know, like a jar for sweets or something. And big! I didn't expect there to be so much volume. It's ground down bones isn't it? I'd never seen human ashes before. They were grey and sort of gritty. I was surprised how unmoved I felt by these ashes, these little bits of rock and dust. I couldn't think of them as Michael, as what remained of him. It was weird.' She fell quiet and stared across the room.

'Anyway,' she collected herself and refocussed her attention on me. 'You asked me about the memorial. So many people came, including his Mum and Dad from Australia. The church was absolutely full. Afterwards we went to a hotel and had a buffet. In fact it was just the same as a funeral except there was no coffin. Everyone was so kind and said lovely things to me about him. Do you know, I had dreaded that day, but when it came, I was sort of on autopilot. Not exactly like I was in Tenerife where I was numb, shocked. It was more... more... I know, it was more that I felt held and supported by all the love around me. And I wanted to do him proud, to give him a fitting tribute. My Michael.

'There were eulogies in the memorial service, saying all sorts of lovely things about his life. The one from Michael's best friend from college actually had us laughing at one point. Not in a disrespectful way, but in a comforting way. He told a story that I'd never heard before about when Michael had just passed his driving test and had bought an old car. He and some friends were going to a festival or something, and they picked up some hitchhikers. Anyway, the handbrake in the car didn't work properly, and Michael couldn't get it to hold on a hill. The hitchhikers said they preferred to walk and got out.'

While she was telling this her face became more animated than I had yet seen it, her cheeks glowed pink and her lips curled into a smile, the first one I'd seen, showing a glimpse of even white teeth. In my notes I had said, *FB showed signs of temporary stimulation and pleasure for the first time when recalling parts of MB's memorial service.* What I did not say was how extraordinarily pretty she looked when she smiled.

Chapter 7

I don't get goatees. OK, if you feel you're not manly enough or whatever and need to have hair on your face, then do it properly. Have a proper, full-on beard like Sean Connery or Jesus. Or like Kai, for that matter. But a bit of hair on your chin and round your mouth... what's that all about? I watched the hairy picture frame around Neville's mouth moving as he spoke and decided that I'd better give some attention to the words that were coming out.

'So as you can see, I truly can envisage The Willows expanding into a comprehensive, forward-looking centre where our clients can get all the help they need with their well-being. Aromatherapy and reiki are two of the obvious additions that we can make to our practice in the medium term.' He was sat back in his office chair, allowing it to swivel from side to side. One leg was resting across the other knee. His immaculate casual trousers were hitched up a couple of inches exposing pale ankle above his lilac-coloured sock and glossily polished shoe. His foot bobbed negligently, out of time with the chair swivelling.

The fact that he'd called me in for a private meeting told me that he saw me as an obstacle to his plans and that he needed to get me on side. 'Already our clients are getting all their mental health requirements met by our team of therapists and counsellors,' I said. 'We have built up a considerable reputation over the years. Whereas aromatherapy and reiki may be acceptable practices in their own right, I believe they simply don't belong with our own. They are alternative therapies and don't directly address mental health, nor are they talking therapies.' We had been batting this particular ball backwards and forwards for the last twenty minutes, both of us remaining ultra-polite, with fixed smiles and studiously open body language. I was sat on the other side of the desk in his room, the room he kept for his own managerial use and his own counselling sessions. Everything in here was more sumptuous than in the rest of the practice, from the deep armchairs with matching sofa to the rich pink velvet curtains. A bit more like a boudoir than a counselling room, if you ask me. I kept my posture relaxed, neither jiggling or tensing any part of my body, and my breathing steady. We were both masters of this particular game.

He wasn't buying my idea – well, Cora's idea – of a client poll on if they would like to see any additions to the practice. We had fenced with that one for a while. He said that he didn't want the clients troubled with complicated, subjective questions; just the standard half a dozen tick boxes that we already had on customer satisfaction was working well.

'You see, Simon,' he changed his position and leant on the desk, his hands reaching out towards me and his expression now more earnest, 'I need you. I need you to help me with this. You are clearly the most experienced, qualified and able therapist here, and I want us to be working in harmony towards common goals. And I've seen how the rest of the staff listen to you.'

When all else fails, turn on the flattery. Did he think I was born yesterday? I side-stepped his appeal and said, 'Apart from the main objection that I've got, namely that these changes are contrary to our ethos, there are other, practical considerations. We would need extra space; at least one extra practice room.'

'Ah,' he smirked and sat back. 'I have given that matter considerable thought. A way forward would be to repurpose the staff room as a space for aromatherapy and reiki and, in fact, any other therapies that we choose to open ourselves to that would require a couch or floor space. It wouldn't take much capital outlay – a good couch, cushions, rugs, that sort of thing. And redecorating, of course.'

He said it all so airily, but I knew he was watching me closely. I didn't lose it, though. I was perfectly calm when I said, 'And what would happen to the current function of the staff room as a place for the staff to take time out between clients, store documents in the filing cabinets, use the kitchen, generally network and chat?'

He waved his hand dismissively. 'The foyer is overlarge for its purpose. We could split it in half with a staff room at the back.'

'A very small staff room with no window. Can you honestly see the staff going for that?'

'It would be adequate.' The veneer was starting to wear thin. 'Look, Simon, there's a lot of extra money to be made by diversifying. We could greatly increase our footfall. They'd come for the bog-standard counselling sessions and then we could flog them a bit of reiki to tag on afterwards. Or vice versa. It's already going down well having Kai here offering hypnotherapy. The word would spread.'

I swear I could almost see the pound signs lighting up in his eyes. So at last he'd come out and admitted it. Money. It was all about money. I was about to counter by asking just how much of these profits would filter down to the staff, when there was a timid knock on the door. Lucy put her head round it and said, 'Sorry to interrupt, but you wanted me to remind you early about your three o'clock so that you could prepare. And she's already here.'

'Thank you, Lucy.' He stood up and I knew I was dismissed. I managed to have the last word on the way out, though. I asked him what would happen to our accreditation with the National Counselling Society if we started peddling all this other stuff. I was bluffing, because I didn't have a clue, but at least I had the satisfaction seeing a worried look flit across his face.

*

The sixth session with Fleur was in a different room. I remember that quite distinctly, although I had not made a note of it (why would I?). For the life of me I can't recall why the room was changed – some booking mix-up, I expect. I never felt quite as much at home in that other counselling room. For a start, it was at the back of the building with a smaller window so there was less light. Then the proportions of the room seemed inappropriate for its use; it was too long and thin, so the chairs and coffee table were disposed awkwardly in the middle with redundant space at either end, which offended me in a strange way. Perhaps I should have taken up feng shui instead of this counselling business. Oh God, don't tell Neville.

She was a few minutes late that day, for the first time. I rechecked my watch, I pottered round the room, I confirmed with Lucy that there hadn't been any messages. I went back to the counselling room and gazed at the bland wall, considering exactly what shade of beige you would call it. Just as I was thinking about messaging her, I heard voices in the lobby. I went out and there she was. Today she was wearing a rain jacket over her signature flowing skirt and blouse, and she carried an umbrella. On her feet she had flat navy-blue shoes with bows on them. Lucy took the jacket and umbrella from her, chatting amiably about the change in the weather. I ushered her in, apologising about the change of location.

'It doesn't matter,' she said. She was slightly breathless and there were vestiges of dampness clinging to her hair. 'I'm sorry I'm a bit late.' She didn't explain why. I was curious, but it would have been intrusive to ask. Maybe she had had difficulty parking. Did she drive here? I didn't know.

I allowed her to settle down, and then I said, 'Fleur, this is the last of the six sessions that you have engaged me for. Of course, this is not the end of the support I hope to give you. We'll need to take out another contract, which Lucy will sort out for you, and then we can continue as we have been. However, I usually take the opportunity at this stage to have a review of what we've achieved so far and where we're going next. How does that sound?' It was a practised speech and I reeled it off.

'OK,' she said. 'But first I have something to say. Some news.'

Her whole demeanour did indeed seem to indicate that she was quietly simmering with a suppressed excitement. She sat

61

forward in her seat, her hands were restless in her lap and she was blinking faster than usual. 'Tell me,' I said.

She took a deep breath, which served as a dramatic pause, and then announced, 'I've decided to go back to El Médano.'

Well, that was unexpected. I took my own deep breath and waited for more.

'I want to take Michael's ashes and scatter them in the sea there. It's where he died, and it just seems right. I think it will help me to forgive myself for not going to his funeral. What do you think?'

'I can see why you might want to do that, but there are several points to consider. Firstly, you have no need of forgiveness for not going to Michael's funeral. We talked about this. While you were so fragile it was a far better thing for you to go home where you would have your family around you, rather than staying in Tenerife on your own. You've had a memorial service which sounded really beautiful and a fitting tribute to his life, and certainly more than served in place of a funeral.' I waited, partly to consider the best phrasing of what I wanted to say and partly to give her time to digest my words. 'Have you considered that it's a very risky strategy, Fleur, going back to El Médano? Being there would allow all those very painful memories to revive and reactivate. It will plunge you directly back into the time of Michael's death and that's probably not a good idea for quite a while. When were you thinking of going?'

'I've booked a flight for three days' time.'

'*Three days' time?*' I wasn't quick enough to keep the surprise and consternation out of my voice.

'Yes. There was just one seat left on the flight so I went for it. I've booked that hotel too, the one I told you about, the one overlooking the sea where I thought I could stay in on my own. I've got a room with a view of the beach and Montaña Roja. I was so lucky to get it at this short notice. That's why I was a bit late today. Once I'd booked the flight I wanted to be sure that the hotel was arranged as well. It's for ten days.' I wondered how much of the uncharacteristic breathless bravado was a front.

I struggled to get my act together in order to respond with something constructive. In my profession you hear extraordinary things, but rarely had I been so taken aback as I was by Fleur's unexpected disclosure. I felt disappointed – alright, annoyed – that she hadn't discussed it with me.

'The thing that decided me was the money, the £50,000,' she said. 'I can afford the trip easily now, and I was due for a couple of weeks annual leave from work.'

I could sense her defensiveness, clearly resulting from the disapproval that I hadn't hidden in time. It would be a setback to lose the trust that we had built up over the weeks, so I strove to steer the discussion away from any confrontation. 'Well, I applaud your initiative. When you first came to see me you wouldn't have been capable of taking such a bold step.'

She acknowledged this. 'When I said it was the money that decided me, I don't only mean that now I have plenty of funds available to make a trip like this. The payout sort of… I don't know… it *validated* Michael's death in a way that nothing else had. It made him really dead. Now I feel I can believe it. It's still hard, though. I miss him.'

She sat quietly after that simple statement. Then she added, 'Do you know what else I've been thinking about this week? The autopsy report said they found water in his lungs. That's why the actual Cause of Death on the Death Certificate was drowning, even though it was the heart attack that must have made him fall in the water in the first place.'

She stopped, obviously struggling with what she wanted to say.

'Take your time,' I said. How many times had I said that to a client?

'I hope… oh, I do hope he didn't suffer for long, panicking alone in the water.' Her face crumpled and she covered it with her hands. 'Would it have taken long for him to die?' Her voice was muffled between her fingers.

'I would think not. He almost certainly had a massive pain in his chest, fell off the board and breathed in water straightaway. It would have been over very quickly, in a matter of seconds.' It was a compassionate response and also probably true.

'Do you really think so?' I reassured her again and passed her a tissue. She wiped her face. 'I used to think about this a lot in the first few weeks. I would tell myself that if he'd been in the water clinging to his board, the helicopter searches would surely have found him. So he must have died straightaway. It's odd that his board and sail were never found, though.'

'Presumably they sank.'

'Yes.' She was calmer now. 'But going back to the money … say he had died straightaway from the heart attack, so that he was dead before he hit the water and therefore didn't drown, then I wouldn't have had that big payout. It wouldn't have qualified as "accidental death".'

'And how do you feel about that?' The counsellor's old cliché.

She considered. 'I can't explain.' She started to initiate her comfort mechanism, picking up the end of her plait, but then she dropped it. 'Strange. Awkward. Undeserving. Guilty.'

'I can understand that.'

'I could give some of the money to a charity. I'll think about it while I'm away. Gosh, in four days' time I'll be there. In El Médano.'

'Have you given any thought to how things will be for you there? It is going to be challenging, you know.'

'Mm. I guess so. That time, the time when Michael died, seems unreal, like a nightmare. And it was all so rushed; once the funeral had been arranged Hugo and I came home. There didn't seem to be any proper goodbye, either to the place or to Michael. I think, I hope, if I scatter his ashes in the sea there, where he died, it will give me some closure. Anyway, it feels like something I have to do. I have to go back. It's, like, I have unfinished business there.' She looked directly at me. 'Does that make sense? Do you understand?'

Another shower was passing through, sucking the light out of the room, and rain spattered noisily up against the window. Another reason I was not so keen on this room.

'Certainly a ritual, a symbolic enactment like scattering ashes, can help with closure. So yes, I understand.'

I cleared my throat and changed my approach. I wanted to get in at least some review of our six sessions. 'You know, you really have made incredible progress since you started seeing me, Fleur.' I shuffled my notes as I went over how distraught she'd been on her first visit to me, and how she'd had to resort to writing down her story in order to get to the stage where she could actually talk about it. Then how we had made rapid progress regarding her acceptance of the reality of Michael's death. She listened impassively, nodding every now and then.

'My concern for you now is that this trip to the place where Michael died might be a setback for you. I wouldn't be fulfilling my role as your counsellor very well if I didn't highlight that. So perhaps we should talk about some coping strategies for while you're away. How does that seem?'

'Alright. I do feel a bit worried about it now.'

So we spent the rest of the session going over how it might feel when she was in El Médano. I sought to stay realistic but positive. We talked through how she envisaged the ashes scattering ceremony, the emotions she was likely to feel and how she could work with them rather than fighting or suppressing them. I encouraged her to write down her thoughts and feelings in her journal, and to use her family back at home as a lifeline if she needed it. Inevitably some of this journey will be incredibly sad, I told her, but not all of it. I then moved on to positive experiences that she would be able to tap into. She would be able to visit places that she loved. She would be able to remember with peace and gratitude the times she had spent there with Michael and now start to have a different perspective on them.

At the end of the conversation she was thoughtful and

solemn, but at least I had tried to make her more prepared. After some hesitation I said that although I wasn't allowed to phone her, if she really needed to, she could phone me on my work mobile. I stressed that this was stretching our rules, because my mobile was only supposed to be used for contact regarding sessions or queries, not for actual counselling. However, I judged that this was a special situation.

I finished on an upbeat note and wished her good luck on her travels. Finally, I suggested that she should book another standard group of six sessions with me, and that we should meet soon after her trip. I stood with her in the foyer while she sorted it all out with Lucy. I watched her fumble in her bag to find her credit card, her face puckered in concentration.

It's too soon, I thought. It's not even a year yet since Michael died. Given the fait accompli that she had presented me with, I'd had to come up with a cobbled together bunch of practical survival suggestions. Yet all my experience told me that this was way too soon. This fragile, ethereal, beautiful woman would be engulfed by an avalanche of emotions. And I wouldn't be around to help her.

Chapter 8

One advantage of living on your own is that you can keep your bike in the living room if you want to. Usually mine lives on the balcony, but yesterday evening when I came back after the midweek ride with the club it had come on to drizzle. So I'd kept the bike inside to do a few minor adjustments and then not bothered to put it out again. I quite like coming home and seeing my bike there. To my mind it doesn't look out of place in the heart of my flat with the telly, sofa, table, books and other general paraphernalia. Tonight though, it struck a wrong note, and I looked with disfavour at the cycling shorts and shoes that I'd peeled off yesterday and left on the floor, along with my cereal bowl and coffee mug. And yes, I did say that I clear my stuff away and wash up every day, but then some days I don't. And today was one of them.

It probably didn't help that I hadn't expected to walk in and see this mess at eleven o'clock at night when I wasn't in the best of moods. The whole slightly sordid scene was not best displayed under the harsh electric light and would have looked better first seen in the daylight tomorrow. I poured myself a whisky and slumped on the sofa, phone in hand. Had she messaged me and I hadn't heard? No.

The evening hadn't gone well from the start. I arrived after work, looking forward to an evening of stimulating chat, Cora's cooking (not her finest point but tolerable), gentle TV and not-so-gentle sex. This would be followed by sex again in the morning before work if I was lucky. It was a formula that worked well for us as a quiet night in the week. This particular time, though, I'd arrived to find Cora dishevelled, which was a contrast to her normal well-groomed turnout. Sometimes dishevelled is OK if it means casual, bohemian, laidback, but Cora's was more the wild, slightly out-of-control type. I put my arms around her for our customary welcome kiss and felt immediately the waves of tension just emanating from her. Whoa.

It turned out that she was having a crisis of confidence about her upcoming exhibition. It's not good enough, it's banal, it's derivative, there's not enough variety, there's no sustained theme, I need to scrap it all and start again, I'll never be ready in time… She was in a real panic. I went into listening mode (my forte, of course) and then soothed her as best I could, both with reassurances and an attempted cuddle, but she wasn't having any of it. Eventually I had to leave her alone and she went to her easel and continued sketching, or whatever she was doing, while I leafed through a book. I enquired tentatively about dinner and she said we'd better order a pizza. The half an hour that they told me when I phoned turned out to be nearer an hour and then I discovered they'd messed my order up and sent pepperoni when I knew I'd ordered Hawaiian. We munched away accompanied by desultory attempts at conversation on my part which eventually trailed away into silence.

By this time I was getting pretty pissed off, and it ended up with me saying I might as well go home. She flew into a rage and threw a book across the room. So I didn't exactly go off in a huff, but there was a distinctly chilly leave-taking. And now here I was, late-night whisky drinking on my own and starting to get melancholy.

The trouble is, I can't say I have any interest in art. I'm a total ignoramus and, to be honest, for all of my thirty-six years I've been quite content to be that way. I look at Cora's stuff and try to say something that isn't completely stupid, but it all looks like coloured daubs to me. Sometimes she will attempt explanations and I try to look interested. Which I am, but only insofar as I am interested in Cora and what makes her tick.

I suppose we had gravitated to a trade-off whereby we both had areas of our respective lives that the other didn't share, namely I didn't usually have to suffer Cora's art thrust in my face and she didn't want to know anything about my family. That did niggle me, though. She wouldn't accept Joe at all, but Nathan was my real son, dammit. The one time I had got all three of us – me, her and Nathan - to meet for a burger had been disastrous. I still cringe with embarrassment when I remember the stilted small talk and my hearty attempts to get us all to relax. I don't know which of those two was the worst. Never again.

I swallowed the last of my whisky and gazed wistfully at the bottom of the empty glass. It was lucky that I'd left the bottle on the other side of the room and I couldn't be arsed to get up. If it had been right beside me I doubt if my glass would have remained empty. Which would not have been a good idea with two new clients back-to-back tomorrow morning and my monthly supervision in the afternoon. Thinking of the day ahead gave me the hook that I needed to stop myself from spiralling down into gloomy speculation. I took a step back and did a bit of self-counselling by mentally evaluating my relationship with Cora. We had plenty of good things going on. We had proper dates going to restaurants, clubs, the cinema, the theatre, concerts, that sort of thing. We interspersed those dates with quiet evenings in. We had good sex. Correction, great sex. We gave each other space to do our own thing; most Sundays I was out with the cycle club, and I saw Nathan practically every week, sometimes twice a week. On weekends she often had parents-visiting duties, which I'd never been asked to participate in, thank God. Neither of us had said the L-word. I had agonised over this when I sent her a birthday card recently. Should I sign it "Love, Simon"? In the end I had chickened out and put "Have a great day, darling. Simon xxxxxxxxx".

Really, she ticked all the good girlfriend boxes – including being one hell of a looker. I pulled out my phone and hesitated. Then I wrote, *Sorry I stomped off like that. I should have been more understanding. I know you're under a lot of pressure right now and I do support you. Forgive me? xxx*. Before sending it I re-read it and changed *should* to *could*.

I was just getting into bed when her reply came: *I'm sorry too. I was overwrought and panicky. Thanks for listening. Are we still on for*

Saturday night? I'll be in a better mood, I promise xxx

Yes, she was a good girlfriend. *I certainly hope we're still on. I'll book somewhere really nice. Goodnight, sexy xxx.* She replied with a kissy lips emoji. I turned over and slept like a log.

*

I had waited with mixed feelings for Fleur to arrive for her seventh session. On the one hand I felt a certain amount of trepidation, yet paradoxically, I was eager to see her. How much would she have been set back by this impulsive pilgrimage to El Médano? Would it have retriggered her disbelief issues? We would need to work through this carefully. During the first few days that she was away I had checked my work mobile several times a day for any messages from her. There had been none. I couldn't know if that was good news or not. I hadn't put any of that in my notes – they were essentially factual - but I do recall those feelings quite distinctly.

What hit me between the eyes when Fleur came in was how tanned she was. The skin on her face and arms was an even golden brown, as if she had been burnished. She was wearing jewellery; an ethnic-looking necklace and dangly earrings that glinted when she moved. And my eye was also caught by a gold ankle bracelet that I'm sure hadn't been there before. It is part of my job to assess the client's outward presentation, which is the first indicator of how they are feeling. My first impression was one of physical wellbeing and care taken in her appearance. A good, if surprising, start. I kept my curiosity in check while she settled herself.

'Welcome back, Fleur. It's good to see you again.' My tone was neutral and I resisted the temptation to jump right in and question her.

She greeted me back. She looked uncertain, hesitant. 'I got back from El Médano yesterday.'

'How was the trip?' An innocuous small sentence to cover a

70

big topic.

She spread her hands. 'I don't know where to start. I haven't had chance to process it all yet.'

'Well, why don't you start from the beginning, the first day. In that way you won't miss anything out. Or, just let it all come out in any order.'

'The first day. I was nervous, flying out there. Why am I doing this, I said to myself. The woman in the seat next to me was the friendly, chatty type, which normally I would have welcomed to pass the time, but I didn't want to talk. I didn't want her asking where I was going and wondering why I was on my own. I buried myself in my book and she took the hint.

'I had gone through it all in my mind beforehand. The view of the coastline as we came in to land, getting the case from the carousel, the taxi ride, the hotel. It seemed odd getting out of the taxi at the Hotel Médano rather than at our apartment. Well, it never was ours, but you know what I mean. I got through the task of checking into the hotel – I even managed a few words in Spanish at the desk – and went up to my room. The bed was vast and white, and I would be sleeping in it on my own. I went out onto the balcony, which was built over the sea, and saw all the people enjoying themselves on the beach and the windsurfers zipping over the waves. Just like Michael used to do. And it hit me just like one of those waves. *He wasn't here.* How could it be, how was it possible, that he wasn't here? The sudden not-hereness of him was overwhelming.'

She was calm and unemotional, as though she'd practiced the speech and had honed her words to convey exactly how she had felt. The not-hereness. 'You could have phoned me,' I said.

'I know. I did think of that, but the truth is I was incapable of doing anything. I lay down on the big white bed and stared at the walls. I'd left the balcony door open and sounds of the waves breaking on the shore and people's voices drifted in to me. I lay there for a long time and then I started to cry. I thought I would never stop. Why, oh why, did I come here, I said to myself. I don't have the words to tell you how awful I felt. It was as bad as when I first came home after he'd died.'

"I told you so" wasn't in my counsellor's vocabulary. And yet... she looked so composed and self-possessed today. I was puzzled. It couldn't be just an illusion created by a suntan, surely. I empathised with her. 'That must have been really painful for you.' Her eyes were downcast and I could see her reliving the episode. 'What happened next?' I prompted.

'Well, eventually I dragged myself off the bed and washed my face. I felt awful – shaky and weak, as if I were ill. I said to myself that I might as well get it all over with, so I put on a pair of big sunglasses to hide my red eyes and I went out. I walked along the seafront and looked at all the little bars that we used to go to. One had changed hands and had a new name, but not much else was different. I walked past the apartment we had stayed in. Wetsuits and towels hung over the railing. I looked inside and saw a woman in shorts doing something at the sink and a baby playing on the floor. It wasn't ours anymore; we might never have stayed there. I saw the lifeguard station and the lifeboat that had gone out to look for Michael. I passed by the windsurfing centre. I stopped outside, but I didn't go in. I ended up in the peaceful little garden of the hotel where the two detectives had come with Michael's watch, where I had signed him away and they had said they were very sorry for my loss. I sat down and ordered a coffee. I had done it all. I had been to all the places that had been part of the story when Michael died.

'I didn't feel so anguished, so completely devastated, as I had felt when I first arrived in the hotel room. Rather I felt numb, exhausted. Yet I had survived the worst shock, the shock of being back there without Michael, and that had its own satisfaction. Perhaps I'm saying that last bit with hindsight? I'm not sure now exactly what I had felt at the time. I know I was deeply sad. But I was used to sad.'

She sighed and brushed her hands together, as if ridding herself of the memory. 'Then I walked back to the hotel and had a long shower. By now it was time for dinner, so I got changed and forced myself to go to the dining room. I'd booked half-board, you see. It was noisy, canteen-like, crowded. Not like the intimate little places where Michael and I used to eat. I did eat something, though, because I knew my body must need food, even though I didn't feel hungry. Then I had a couple of drinks in a bar and wondered how I was going to get through the next nine days. I did actually sleep quite well that night. I think that was because I was drained with all the emotion. It also helped that I left the window open and the sound of the little waves lapping onto the shore was right underneath me. It was a comforting sound.

'The next day, after breakfast, I unpacked my things. It really was quite a nice room, as hotel rooms go. Not very big – it would have been quite small for two – but clean and full of light. And the view of the beach, the sea, and Montaña Roja was amazing. Yet I found it disorienting. You see, I already knew this view so well and loved it. It couldn't have changed of course, and yet it was subtly different – everything was different - because Michael wasn't there. Then I realised that the change was in me. I myself had changed.

'I thought about this over the next few days. It mirrored how I felt about my house. In the early days it was excruciating to be living there. It was supposed to be *our* house, mine and Michael's, our home. We had bought it together, furnished it together, lived in it together. And now he had gone away. The house, which seemed so big and lonely in the early days and a constant reminder of my loss, had gradually become *my* house. Over the months I had replaced many of Michael's things with my own. I had redecorated. I had mentally grown into it and allowed it to shelter and hold me. In El Médano I did a lot of thinking about that and other things. I could look back over these months and realise how far I had come. Does that make any sense?'

I validated what she had shared with me. 'The fact that you

had physically distanced yourself from your daily life had enabled you to view your progress over the last few months objectively,' I told her, in counsellor-speak. I was still reserving my opinion and apprehensions regarding this epiphany of hers.

'Anyway, I'm getting ahead of myself,' she continued. 'So much happened. Let's see, I'll try to tell it in the order it happened. On the second day I took Michael's ashes and scattered them on the shore so that the incoming tide could take them. I'd waited until just after dark, so that no-one could see what I was doing. Putting his ashes there felt like exactly the right thing to do. He had died there, and so it was a fitting place to put his remains. It was sad, but strangely comforting too. It would have been worth going back to El Médano just for that.

'The other thing I knew I wanted to do was to see Hans. So on the third day I walked down to the windsurfing centre to see if I could catch him for a quick chat. Already, walking past all the landmarks was less traumatic than it had been the previous day. Hans was delighted to see me and I was able to thank him for his help last year with all the translation. His business was doing well and I was pleased about that. He asked me how I was coping and said how well I looked, which was kind of him, because I suspect I actually looked a bit frazzled. After a few minutes of this we didn't really have anything else to say to each other, and he was busy, so I took my leave. Another box ticked.

'By the third day I was getting used to the dining room in the hotel. It was a magnificent room, light and airy, built out on this pier over the sea, so it had sea views on three sides. The food was plentiful and well prepared, and you helped yourself to whatever you wanted. At first I was very self-conscious, being on my own. I thought everyone would be looking at me pityingly. But in fact, no-one was particularly interested. I also noticed that I wasn't the only singleton. There were five other people eating on their own. It's funny, when you're in a couple, lone people are invisible to you. Had there been people on their own when Michael and I had eaten out? I never noticed. There was one woman who was particularly gregarious. She would be about fifty, I would say, she walked with a stick, and she was on her own. As she made her slow progress past with her plate from the buffet, she would stop and chat to everyone on her way back to her table. This fascinated me. She was so cheerful and outgoing, and not the least bit shy. I found myself wanting her to stop at my table. All I had to do was look up, catch her eye and smile and she did.'

This reaching out was an unexpected development. I began to see how Fleur had tapped into a source of positivity and support. I sat back, absorbed in her narrative, while she told me about how she had struck up a friendship with this lady, who was called Hilary. They had expanded their little circle to include Niels, who was from Denmark. She described how the trio had drinks most days after dinner, and sometimes met up in the afternoon too. The other two had lost their respective partners a couple of years ago (Niels's partner was a man). 'I realised,' said Fleur, 'that all the people I associated with at home were people I had known before Michael died. I had no new friends, neither did I have contact with anyone who had also been widowed. I hit it off with Hilary and Niels, and we were able to talk to each other quite openly about our bereavements, living alone and lots of other things. Which was surprising, since on the face of it we didn't have anything in common.'

'Yet if you think about it, you had two crucial things in common. You had all had the experience of a partner's death and you had all chosen to stay at the Hotel Médano.'

I could see her mulling this over. Then she said suddenly, 'Do you remember when I told you all about the day Michael died? How I had sat in a bar just off the plaza and I looked up at the Hotel Médano and thought that if I was on my own, I would stay there? Well, it turned out to be true, didn't it. Both being on my own and me staying there. Don't you think that's spooky?'

'Not spooky in itself. Everything, when we look at it from the correct perspective, has a rational explanation. On the day in question you were, by your own admission, feeling slightly annoyed with Michael. You probably subconsciously noticed some people on their own going into the hotel. And you've described it as a very attractive looking hotel.'

'I suppose so,' she said, sounding unconvinced.

'Fleur, you really have been tremendously brave, you know. It took a lot of courage to engage with the pain of revisiting El Médano. It was a bold gamble because it might not have turned out so well for you. And you have made a big step forward not only in your grieving, but in establishing new relationships.' I paused. I wanted to phrase the next bit exactly right. 'You're clearly rather elated now, and so you should be. But with such a big advance often comes the risk of your emotional pendulum swinging back too far the other way, which can be quite bewildering and frightening, before it settles back to somewhere in the middle. We can work on that in the forthcoming weeks.'

'Thank you, but I don't think I'm going to come back again after today.'

For a minute I didn't quite take in what she'd said. I really hadn't seen that coming. 'I would advise that's an unwise course of action. As I have said, you're almost certainly going to come down from all the excitement-'

'Simon, I appreciate what you're saying, but I really don't want to be thinking about that pathetic person I was when I first came here. And when I came into this room, it reminded me.'

I tried everything to persuade her to change her mind. I mentioned that it was coming up to the first anniversary of Michael's death, which might well provoke disturbing memories. But her opinion was that those memories had already been taken care of in El Médano, so the anniversary wasn't going to signify in the way it might have done.

When she left we shook hands and she said, 'I went to El Médano as a widow. I've returned as a single person. Thank you so much for all the help you've given me over these weeks, Simon. I couldn't have done it without you.' She gave me a big smile and was gone.

There was nothing more I could do. I had an hour before my next client so I went for a walk to the green area around the corner. I sat on the bench and watched a woman with a small child on her lap. I pulled out my phone, my go-to distraction technique, and the memory of a conversation I'd had with a woman in a wine bar a couple of nights ago came back into my mind. We'd swapped phone numbers, but I couldn't remember her name. I messaged her anyway and asked if she fancied a drink that night. While I was walking back to work her reply came through: *'OK. I'll meet you at the same wine bar at 8.30pm. Cora.'*

Chapter 9

Some of my colleagues groan at the thought of their compulsory monthly supervision, but I have always valued it. It does exactly what it says on the tin: you get a safe and supportive opportunity to reflect on how you're progressing with your clients, you get impartial suggestions and guidance, you get a chance to air your thoughts and feelings. It's a luxury for me to be doing most of the talking and to be listened to, rather than the other way around, which is how I spend most of my working life. And my supervision sessions are usually at 2pm on a Friday afternoon at Daphne's house, so I get to start my weekend early. What's not to like?

Not that sessions with Daphne are in any way relaxing. She really puts me through my paces. As well as my offloading all the frustrations and issues of the last month, for me it's still an hour and a half of questioning, evaluating and learning. Yes, even after ten years I'm still learning. Perhaps that's one reason why I like my job so much.

Whereas I would always choose to have supervision voluntarily, for us psychotherapists it's actually a professional requirement to attend regular, formal supervision in order to keep our license to practice. For one thing what we hear can be harrowing and could mess with your head if you let it. Also you sometimes need a person with an objective view to step in and give an opinion or even intervene, especially on ethical or safeguarding matters. I remember talking about this with Cora in our early days. She had asked me what the difference was between your line manager and your supervisor, and why one person couldn't fulfil both roles. I explained that the roles are different because you need someone impartial, someone outside the game. She related to it better when I said a supervisor is more akin to a mentor, because she'd been involved with a mentoring scheme in her job. However, mentoring involves only you and the mentor whereas with supervision there is joint focus on the client as well. I often think it must be tough for workers in other professions who don't have this opportunity for self-care and career guidance.

It's a twenty-minute walk from The Willows to Daphne's house, which serves to get me into the zone. Even though I have it all in my notebook, during this time I usually have a mental run-through of my caseload and I put it in a suitable order to talk about. As well as sketching out the story for each, I list any points that I want to clarify, any aspects for discussion, and I try to second-guess any questions that Daphne might have. Not that I'm usually right about that.

I turned into the drive to her house. She's got an elegant, solid-looking place, set back from the road, with an abundance of trees and shrubs in the garden. It gives it a secluded feeling, like being hidden in a wood. I get the impression that it must have been her late husband who'd had the well-paid job, to have a place like this. You don't earn that sort of money working in psychotherapy, trust me. Not that she talks about her husband. In fact, I know very little about Daphne, despite having had her as my first supervisor when I started at The Willows more than a decade ago. After that I had a couple of different supervisors, like you're supposed to, and now I'm back with Daphne again. She knows several things about my life outside work, just enough to colour me in, so to speak, but she has never encouraged questions about her own private life. I know that's appropriate practice for a supervisor, but I would be curious to learn more than just that she has spent all her working life in the talking therapies, that she retired six years ago when her health declined and now she just keeps on a handful of supervisees. I've never seen any photographs or other clues in her house about a family.

The doorbell gave an old-fashioned low 'ding-dong' within the house and I stood under the wooden porch in quiet anticipation. I was used to waiting a few minutes while Daphne shuffled her way to the door. The way her face creased into a smile when she saw me was reassuringly predictable. 'Hello, Simon. Do come in. We're in the snug, as usual.'

I followed her slow progress, which she aided with her walking stick, to the back of the house. We passed the lounge to the left, where the door was open to expose a sumptuous three-piece suite and feature fireplace, and the dining room to the right with a polished table and six chairs arranged at precise distances around it. The snug itself was a small, cosy space, worthy of the name. This was Daphne's supervision room, set up in classical style with two armchairs not quite opposite each other and a side table with water and glasses. Through the window you could see a bird bath in the back garden.

Daphne herself exuded a quiet sophistication which matched her home. She always wore a knee-length tweedy skirt and a plain blouse, usually with pearls or a brooch. On her fingers, knotted now with arthritis, were a couple of large rings set with stones. Family heirlooms, you might imagine. Her short grey hair was always neatly arranged. I do tend to notice what people wear, and how they look. Not a very masculine attribute, you might think, but it's one of the things psychotherapists do. I wonder if others observe me in the same way, and what they make of my conservative trousers and plain open-necked shirt, non-flashy lace-up shoes and a neat haircut. Conventional and middle-of-the-road, I expect.

I settled myself comfortably and took out my notes. Daphne had her own notebook and pen on a side table next to her chair. She never did much writing while I was talking. During those times she sat motionless with her hands folded in her lap, perfectly focused on me and what I was communicating. She would make brief notes, which I expect she amplified later on, between my presentation of each client.

We started, as usual, with her asking me how I was, and if there was anything in my life that I needed or wanted to talk about before we started on the clients. I have always been impressed that she enquired briefly about the significant people in my life, even remembering Nathan and Joe's names. All this wasn't being nosy. Firstly, it was a time for settling down and reaffirming the trust that we have in each other. Secondly, if you have issues in your own life, these could impact negatively on your interactions with clients and so it's recommended that you air them with your supervisor. After these introductory parts, we then passed on to the general situation at the practice, that is, the 'working environment'. I told her about Kai's arrival, and that at first I'd been wary of the idea of hypnotherapy, but I'd warmed to it. She pursued that a bit. I decided not to divulge the friction with Neville, because if I did, she'd be on it straightaway. Cora's comments about alpha males still rankled slightly, and I didn't want Daphne to pick up on that. I decided to leave it until next month when things might have developed more. Anyway, there was enough on today's agenda to be going on with.

It wasn't until I was half-way through a report of my first client, a woman with whom I'd been working for three sessions so far, that we had our customary interruption. Yes, I'd said that I had Daphne's undivided attention when I was talking, which was true until Montagu put in an appearance. Montagu was Daphne's enormous cat. I couldn't tell you what type, because I'm not up on these things, but it was a long-haired, gingery coloured creature with a disdainful expression. It's funny that Daphne is such a model supervisor in every way, except when that cat marches in. Although her attention is supposed to be wholly on what I am saying, I can tell that she is aware of him strutting about and licking his paws. Or worse. Then, having rested his gaze on me and communicated his dislike, he marches out again. Daphne had explained that if she shut him out he'd only yowl and scratch the door until he'd come and had a look at me. Well, we can't have that.

It's up to me in which order I choose to present my clients. What I tend to do is get a couple of uncomplicated ones out of the way first, then sandwich any challenging or potentially contentious cases in the middle and finish up with more easy ones at the end. Today the filling in my sandwich was a case that was going to stretch me somewhat. Initially, this middle-aged man had come to me after his wife had died, and it had all the signs of being a fairly standard scenario of the grief, pain and disorientation that comes with losing someone close to you. My bread-and-butter, in fact. I don't mean to sound blasé, but I would say about half my clients come with pretty straightforward death-related issues like this, which generally respond well to talk and time. We tiptoe around death in our society, and so when it does arrive, it can render people poleaxed with bewilderment and suffering. I help them to normalise their pain. The other half of my clients have more complex grief issues or sometimes non-death related loss issues. Anything else I would pass to my colleagues who have other specialisms.

Anyway, I had seen this particular man four times, and I was getting a growing sense that I was only dealing with the tip of the iceberg. Last time I had gained his trust enough for him to start opening up, right at the end of the session. What started to come out was an unusual story of abuse - his wife abusing him, that was - that had been swept under the carpet for years. Daphne helped me to talk through how I might take this forward, and my own feelings about it. Even ten years on, I've still not 'seen it all'. Poor man. And his poor wife.

In the final twenty minutes or so of the session Daphne usually winds up with taking a look at what's upcoming for me in terms of the clients I'm already seeing, or new ones, or anything else that's relevant. So I mentioned the cryptic phone call that I'd had from Fleur saying that 'he'd come back', and that I'd arranged to see her next week.

'To briefly recap,' I said, 'I had seven sessions with this client last year, which terminated at her request because she felt she no longer needed my support. Her husband had died from having a heart attack while windsurfing during a holiday in Tenerife, and the key feature in her presentation to me was her difficulty in actualising the death. It would seem that these difficulties have resurfaced.'

'I remember it well,' said Daphne. She said nothing more, but maintained a tactical silence. I shifted in my seat, giving myself away, and I cursed under my breath.

She broke the silence by saying, 'I need to get my notebook from last year. Will you excuse me a moment?'

I heard the sound of a filing cabinet drawer being opened from within another room. I was favoured by another visit from Montagu, who took advantage of Daphne's absence to sashay in and stare at me again. Montagu was around back in my early days with Daphne, so he must be getting on a bit now. I remembered my first visit to Daphne's house when I had been foolish enough, while she was out of the room, to attempt to stroke him. The flash of claws had been like lightening, and two sharp scratches on the back of my hand oozed blood. I had managed to get the wounds wrapped in my handkerchief before Daphne came back, and I spent the rest of the session with my hand secreted down the side of the chair.

Daphne had her finger in a page of her last year's notebook when she came back. She put on her half-moon spectacles which were dangling from a gold chain around her neck, frowning slightly as she read through the pages. When she had finished she looked at me over the top of her glasses. 'I would recommend that one of your colleagues sees this client rather than you.'

I hadn't expected her to be so blunt. 'The client specifically asked for me.' I tried not to sound defensive.

'The question is, as always, what is in the best interests of the client, would you say?'

'To see me, of course, because I have all the background and details of her case. You may not have had time to look back at all the history. The client was experiencing feelings of guilt because she had not seen her husband's body after his death and neither did she attend the funeral. This culminated in her uncertainty that the body which had been found was his. These feelings were only completely allayed - or so it seemed at the time

– when she received an insurance settlement of £50,000 in respect of his accidental death. Then she made the sudden announcement, which she had not discussed with me, to return to the scene of his death. At the time this risky strategy seemed to pay off, because she returned with every appearance of having resolved her issues. She was feeling so recovered that she decided she didn't need any more sessions with me. I did voice my concerns that it was too soon and too abrupt to simply remove the support, but the decision was hers.'

Daphne gave me one of her extended looks. This was a thoughtful, penetrating gaze that seemed to see right down into my soul. It was difficult to keep impassive under this scrutiny. In another life, Daphne would have made a good detective.

Then she said, 'I'm wondering if it's possible that your client cancelled the rest of her sessions because she felt uncomfortable with you.'

I gasped. 'Absolutely not! The client gave every indication that she trusted me completely. After all, she has asked to see me again.' Daphne was definitely adding two and two together and making five. I made an effort to control my indignation by calming my breathing.

Daphne made a quizzical "hmm" sound and referred back to her notes. After a couple of minutes' perusal she looked straight at me and said, 'Do you think the client was aware of the countertransference that was developing?'

I was flabbergasted. She had said the c-word. Every therapist is aware of the professional and personal dangers of emotional entanglement with a client. It's drummed into you during your training. And it happens; you just have to nip it in the bud when it does. It can often be in response to transference from the client. I've really only had one occurrence of it in my career, which was a few years ago when I had a client who had started to flirt with me. Not overtly, just in her posture and manner. Then she started throwing in a few inviting remarks. To my horror I felt myself responding, and before I knew it I was

84

invaded by sexual thoughts about her. I discussed this with Daphne, and she talked me through how to deal with it. The next time I saw the client I told her I was aware that there was a sexual current starting to develop between us, and that we would have to put it firmly aside if we were to continue working together. It worked, and we successfully finished our sessions.

But that was entirely different to the relationship –an entirely professional relationship – that I'd had with Fleur. 'You and I didn't discuss countertransference,' I said.

'No, we didn't. I was ready to explore the subject with you when you came to supervision and reported that the client had terminated the sessions. When we talked about why that was, I did give you my opinion that you seemed overly concerned about the client's welfare, and perhaps overprotective and controlling.'

'I don't remember that.'

'I do have it here in my notes, Simon.' She was quiet and politely firm, as ever. 'I decided not to pursue it because you told me that the sessions had ended. I simply advised you to be careful with your boundaries in the future.'

I really didn't have any recollection of that conversation. But if she had it down in her notebook in black and white I suppose we must have had it. We talk about so many things.

'Alright,' I said. There was no benefit in getting on the wrong side of your supervisor. 'I will make sure that I maintain robust boundaries. My meetings with the client last year resulted in quite dramatic progress so I genuinely feel that I'm the right person to work with her again. And frankly, it's an interesting case and I'm curious to see what has triggered this regression.'

She studied me for a couple of minutes while I did my best to remain impassive. 'Very well,' she said, apparently making her mind up. 'You're an experienced counsellor, Simon, so it's your decision. I hope that after this conversation you'll be particularly alert to any emotional responses on your part in your dealings with this client.'

Normally I feel good after my monthly session with

Daphne. Cleansed and renewed and buzzing with enthusiasm for the profession that I love. But today I felt wrong-footed and furtive, like a caught-out schoolboy.

Chapter 10

Kai was slouched against the draining board in the staff room, staring into a mug of coffee when I walked in. 'You look gloomy. What's up?' I said.

He straightened up and put his mug down on the table. 'Oh, nothing really. It's just that I rushed to get here only to find that my ten o'clock has cancelled.'

'That's a bummer,' I said, helping myself from the pot of coffee that Lucy prepared every morning, and sitting down at the table. 'Luckily it doesn't very often happen at such short notice.'

Kai grunted. 'I had a date last night and I could have done with some extra sleep.'

I inspected him. He did look a bit bleary. Since he obviously wanted me to, I asked him about the date and he filled me in on the drinking, the clubbing and the sex afterwards.

'So internet dating seems to be working out for you. How many women has it been now?'

'Dunno. About half a dozen.'

'Well, good for you.' Who was I to judge?

'She's been to a solicitor about starting divorce proceedings. I got a letter this morning.'

'Ah.' So that's really what he was down in the dumps about.

He shrugged and folded his arms. 'If that's what she wants, let her carry on. As long as I can still get to see my boy.'

I hesitated. 'Look Kai, I know this isn't my business, but seeing your son every other weekend doesn't work out to be as straightforward as you think it will at the beginning. I wish I could see Nathan every day, just to ask how his day's been in school, or whatever. Even though nowadays it's all quite flexible about when I visit, it's still only that – a visit. I often feel out of the loop. And when he comes to me I can tell that sometimes he's bored, but too polite to say. It's an emotional challenge to me and God knows what it's done to him. And, mate, I'm not telling you what to do, but you might want to be careful about all these women you're shagging, until you're divorced.'

I thought he might tell me to sod off and stop interfering, but he sighed and said, 'Yeah. I hear you. Would you have got divorced if you had your time over again?'

Before I had chance to reply Emma and Stacey came into the staff room. We all exchanged chirpy Monday morning pleasantries over steaming mugs, including sharing what we'd done on the weekend. Stacey had been to a festival and Emma had taken delivery of a new dishwasher. Her kids had moaned when she said they had to help stack it. Thankfully Kai had decided to edit his description of his weekend compared to what he'd told me, and instead he reported a trip to a theme park with his son.

Stacey turned to me and beamed. 'And how was your weekend, Simon?' I thought she had some of the festival glow still about her. Love and peace, man. But I shouldn't be cynical; Stacey always tends to be one of the happy people, and that's good.

How was my weekend… It had been mixed, actually. The good bits were a terrific date with Cora on Saturday evening, when we had both been determined to be on our best behaviour, and a great day out with the cycling club on Sunday with a few drinks afterwards. The less good bit was that my car, my trusty Honda Civic that I'd had for seven years, had failed its MOT on Saturday morning. I decided to share the brilliant cycling trip, balanced up with the MOT failure, with the others.

'I didn't know you had a car,' said Emma. 'You always come to work by train, don't you?'

I told them that train made sense from where I live, but I hung onto the car for shopping, visiting family, the odd trip to the countryside, things like that. I didn't use it much, though.

Stacey, ever the environmentalist, nodded her approval as she and Emma stood up to leave. 'You can easily do without a car, living around here,' she said.

Kai enquired what my car had failed the MOT on. I filled him in on the details of two front tyres down to the minimum tread and badly worn brake pads. We shook our heads sadly. 'I wonder if Stacey has a point, and I should consider getting rid of it,' I said.

'Or,' said Kai, poking me in the chest and grinning, 'You could get it fixed and then trade it in for something more sporty.'

'Think I'm made of money, do you?'

'Come off it, you're doing OK. And think what a nice little convertible could do for your image.'

I gathered up my stuff and left him to his fantasies. He was projecting his own desires onto me, probably. Or did he really mean that compared to his loud shirts, long hair and multiple women I was a bit boring and heading towards an early middle age?

*

I forgot Kai and his insinuations as soon as I went into the counselling room and got into the zone with the help of some deep breathing. Yes, I was nervous. It was nine months since I'd seen Fleur, yet reading her notes had brought it all back as fresh as if it were only last week. I left the door open so that I would be forewarned of her arrival, and as soon as I heard the low hum of her voice in conversation with Lucy I jumped up, wiping my palms on my trousers, and headed out to the foyer to greet her. She turned around as she heard me walk up behind her.

I couldn't help it. I just gasped and out it came. 'Your hair! What have you done to your hair?'

'My hair? Oh, I decided to cut it all off.' She seemed a bit embarrassed at my reaction and I can't say I blamed her. Her Rapunzel-like tresses were totally gone and instead her hair was cropped short all over.

Lucy saved the day by chiming in with, 'My friend had really long hair and she's just had it cut off for charity. I thought it was a really generous thing to do.'

Fleur ran her hand over her skullcap of hair. 'I gave mine to a charity too.'

'Would you like to come through,' I said, more loudly than I'd intended. 'I expect you remember the way.'

I allowed her to go ahead of me. After one glance I averted my eyes from the pale nape of her neck, exposed by the scoop neckline of her summery top. I shuffled my notes as she settled herself in the chair. I sat back with my notebook on my knee, crossed my legs loosely and pasted a pleasant, neutral expression on my face. I was experienced enough to know how to play the part of the counsellor no matter what might be going on inside me.

'Well, Fleur, it's been quite a while since we last met. How have things been for you?'

'I don't know where to start. It's been quite a journey. I thought I was moving forward until the last few weeks.'

I nodded in acknowledgment. I had no intention of diving straight in to quiz her about the message that she had left.

'Before we get started,' I said, 'I need you to fill in another form, just like you did last year. It's the same standard information about your address, any medication, how you are generally feeling, that sort of thing.'

She bent her head over the clipboard as she wrote. Her lips were parted and she was frowning slightly in concentration. I took the opportunity, while she was looking down, to stare at her and to absorb the shock of her new hairstyle. It was barely two inches long all over. Not that I know much about these things, but I guess it must have been done by an expert stylist since it managed to make her look both sophisticated and elfin at the same time. I pictured the severed plait, lying like a dead snake on a floor somewhere. By now it had probably found a new life as wigs for chemotherapy patients who had lost their hair. I wondered if she still felt its presence, as an amputee might experience a phantom limb. What did her hands do now when she was stressed or agitated, when there was no heavy coil of hair to stroke?

I cast my eye briefly over the form when she passed it back. I saw that she had intermittently been prescribed medication for insomnia and that her address was different. I commented on this.

'Yes,' she replied. 'I eventually moved house a month ago. It took a long time to find somewhere that I liked, then the sale of my house fell through and I had to start all over. Then when I found a buyer again I quickly had to find somewhere for me to buy. I'd heard what a nightmare it can be when you're in one of these chains, and it's certainly true. The new place is about ten miles away from my old house. That makes it a bit further away from work, but it's OK.'

I made a mental note that she didn't sound entirely happy about the house move and that I should pick up on that. While I was mentally framing my gambit she abruptly changed the subject and said, 'When I phoned and left that message I'd panicked. You see, I was in the park near my house when I saw him. He was walking with a dog on a lead, some sort of black spaniel. Michael always loved dogs, especially the spaniel type. You know, the lively ones. We used to talk about getting a puppy, but we decided it wouldn't really be fair since we were both out all day.

'I only saw him from the back, but he had the build, the way of walking, the balding head of Michael. He was, oh I don't know, about twenty metres away from me and he was about to turn and go out of the gates. I jumped up from the bench where I was sitting and ran after him, weaving through the people. But when I got to the park gates he'd disappeared. I looked frantically up and down the street and then I caught a glimpse of him in a red car, just pulling out from the curb, driving away from me.'

I took a moment to marvel inwardly at how all women seem to identify cars by their colours. 'I went and sat back down on the bench. I was shaking. It had just come out of the blue and it really disturbed me. That's when I phoned you.'

She was twisting her fingers in her lap. So that's what she did when she was anxious, now that her long plait was gone. I noticed that she no longer wore her wedding ring and engagement ring.

'Let me see if I've got the time sequence right. This happened nearly three weeks ago, so it was about a week after you moved house?' She nodded. 'And have you seen this person again since then?'

She shook her head. 'No. I've been away for part of that time. I mentioned when you phoned me that I was going on a family holiday to celebrate my parents' ruby wedding. I've been back to the park four times, at roughly the same time of day, but I haven't see him.' She leaned forward. 'Simon, it couldn't possibly be him, could it? Not after eighteen months, surely. I haven't been able to sleep, worrying about it.'

I sought to reassure her and normalise her reactions. 'No. He certainly wasn't Michael. But I can understand how unsettling it was, seeing someone who reminded you of him. Your conscious mind – your common sense - told you that it couldn't possibly be Michael, because you know he's dead, but your unconscious registered only that here was someone who matched your husband in appearance. Yet logically you knew it was impossible, and hence your confusion and mismatch between your conscious and unconscious mind. All this was made worse because of your feelings when you first came to see me – that you believed at that time that Michael might not be dead.'

I could see her digesting this. 'Do you know what I keep thinking?' she said. 'What would it be like if it *was* him? What if Michael came back into my life, right now? Half of me thinks how wonderful that would be, we could pick up where we left off, and the other half of me feels scared and shies away from it. How can that be, given that I loved him so much? I'm so mixed up.'

She was getting quite agitated. I could see her chest moving up and down as her breathing quickened. The first thing I needed to do was to reach into her turmoil and soothe her. 'Having conflicting emotions is very disturbing, isn't it? The first thing to accept – completely accept - is that the man you saw *was not* Michael. Michael cannot possibly come back. It's a bit like having a nightmare, particularly a recurring nightmare. While you know it isn't real, it's still frightening when it happens.'

That seemed to go some way towards calming her. 'I used to get bad dreams where Michael was there but in some way he wasn't quite himself. And then I would realise he was dead. After I woke up I would tell myself it was just a dream, but it would take me a time to shake off the feeling. I don't get those dreams now.'

'Exactly. And that's what's happening now. You can think of your experience seeing the Michael look-alike just as if it were a bad dream. The other thing, Fleur, is that people who have been widowed a year or so often go through the contradictory thought process that you just described, namely that they speculate on what it would be like if their spouse came back.'

She looked puzzled, so I elaborated. 'When a person is moving through the grieving process, what we see generally is that their everyday life experiences alternate between 'loss-oriented' processes, such as feeling sad, and 'restoration-oriented' processes such as doing new things. Gradually restoration experiences come to predominate. When the individual has moved beyond grieving and has constructed a satisfactory modified life for themselves that no longer includes their partner, it causes confusion to think of how the dead person would fit into this new life. It is actually quite a good sign. It means that the recovery phase has been well established. I've encountered countless instances of this behaviour pattern in my work.' I wouldn't actually say countless, but I thought it didn't hurt to stretch a point here.

'So you mean…' she faltered and looked cautious.

'I mean it's OK to feel perplexed and upset like you were. It

was normal. It *is* normal. You can accept it and let it pass now.'
I paused. 'Would you like some water?'

She accepted and sat back to sip from the glass. Likewise I
sat back and allowed her time to absorb all this. I allowed her to
rest in the nurturing silence. I could actually observe her relaxing
– her shoulders dropped and the lines on her face smoothed out.
I mentally gave myself a pat on the back. Apart from the radical
new hairdo, I noted that she looked much the same as last year
– neat, feminine and slightly vulnerable. One small difference
was that the trademark long skirt had been replaced by loose
cotton trousers that finished mid-calf, showing off her slim
ankles.

She said, 'Moving house has been stressful. More stressful
than I thought it would be, and I'm by no means settled in yet.'

'Moving house is often cited as one of the most demanding
things that happens in our lives.'

She sighed. 'At first I thought I'd made a big mistake. You
see, it was a huge scramble to find somewhere else after first sale
fell through. I'm still trying to get used to the new place. I
suppose it's getting a bit less strange now.'

'It is a big change to move to a new home in a new area. Be
gentle with yourself and allow time to adjust. I'm going to suggest
that we use the rest of the session today for you to start telling
me what has happened in your life since we last met. How does
that sound?'

She agreed, and I settled down to absorb her story.

It turned out, she told me, that the slightly euphoric
confidence that she had displayed the last time she saw me didn't
last. The pendulum of her mood swung back and during the next
few weeks she struggled to regain the feeling that her life was
moving forwards. I nodded inwardly; it was exactly as I would
have predicted. She spoke of seeing more of her friends and
joining a Pilates class where she made new ones. The marriage
of one of her oldest friends had broken up, and they formed an
alliance for going out and for discussing and comparing their

situations. 'I know that getting divorced isn't the same process as being widowed,' she said. 'But the end result is the same. You're on your own and trying to find ways to cope. Also it helped me with my own challenges to be focussing on hers instead. We supported each other.' I said that I thought this friendship was a good thing for her.

It was this friend who had talked about moving house, which had raised it as a possibility for Fleur herself. 'At first I rejected the idea out of hand,' she said. 'I'd lived there since we got married, and the thought of moving and living somewhere else was overwhelming. But, on the other hand, the house was now too big for me. And I could see that a new house, which would be wholly mine, would give me a fresh start. If that was what I wanted. You see, it meant leaving memories of Michael behind. Sometimes those memories were a torment, and sometimes they were a comfort. I used to talk to Michael in the house. Would I still be able to talk to him somewhere else? Would I want to? Or would I forget him? I didn't feel ready for that.'

I was sorry that I had not been supporting Fleur at the time she was going through these contradictory emotions. The feelings and choices themselves, that is, clinging to the safe past or embracing an uncertain future, were the standard dilemmas that faced widowed people thinking of uprooting themselves to a new home. This is why it's usually not a good idea to move house until, as a rule of thumb, after about a year of bereavement. I told her all this, and that she seemed to have handled the issues admirably for herself and congratulated her that she'd had the courage to move forward.

She made a face. 'Yes and no. Although it is reassuring to know you think I'm doing OK, thank you. The thing is, I had quite warmed to the first house that I chose, and I'd decided that it was the right thing for me to do – part of the closure, if you like. Then there was all the hassle of the deal falling through and I ended up being rushed. I don't feel I'm warming to the house

I chose. I thought that to change where I live would be a huge step forward for me in terms of personal growth. But it's not like that... it feels strange. There's nothing intrinsically wrong with the house itself, or the location. It's just that it doesn't feel *me*.'

I questioned her about what it was that didn't feel right, but she couldn't put her finger on it. I then ventured the opinion that her strong reaction to seeing the Michael-like man was linked to her feelings of not yet being grounded in her new home. She nodded slowly, so I knew she had taken the idea on board as a possibility.

'We can talk more about this next week,' I said, 'But before you go let me give you a couple of thoughts to mull over and help you until then. Firstly, it's early days. You've been in the house less than a month, and so it's probably unrealistic to expect complete adaptation to your new environment already. Secondly, we can help ourselves a lot by accepting what can't easily be changed. It's a fact that this is now where you live, so do you think you could consciously seek out the good points, and look at ways to personalise the house? Don't resist your difficult feelings but give it time and gentle willingness.'

I think I'd got through to her, judging by her thoughtful expression. She was so rewarding to work with. Her emotions were transparent, she articulated her struggles clearly and she listened to my comments. She brought out the best in me as a counsellor. I wanted to reach out and hold her hand. Instead, I said 'You are doing so well, you know Fleur. I can see how much you have grown around your grief, as we say. You have worked through the pain and allowed it to enrich you as a person.'

She was quite taken aback by this remark and didn't know what to say. Before I could stop myself I blurted out, 'Why did you cut your hair?'

She was surprised by the question. 'Oh, the friend I mentioned brought it up. She said that you could give long hair to charity and I thought it would be symbolic of my changing life. A new appearance for a new chapter.' She smoothed her hands over her head. 'I don't think about it now. You'd think I'd miss it, but I don't. All that hair took a lot of looking after. I feel much lighter now.'

She didn't seem unduly disconcerted about a question that slightly contravened the boundaries of our relationship. We said our goodbyes, I showed her out and then returned to the counselling room, which I knew wasn't booked for the next hour. I gazed at the chair where she had sat while I tried to collect my unruly thoughts. Daphne was right. For that matter, so was Neville, which was more annoying. I should not have taken Fleur Bentley on as a client again.

Chapter 11

The thought that Kai had planted had been ticking away in the back of my mind for a few days. Did I actually need a fancy sports car? No. Did I want one? Maybe. A bit of online research told me that Thursday was the day that my nearest BMW garage stayed open until the evening, so I figured it would do no harm to have a drive over there after work, just to have a look.

I was aware of how puny my Honda looked in the car park compared to the sleek muscle of most cars there. Even the ones not for sale were a cut above mine. I sauntered into the showroom, trying my best to look cool, although I was aware that my conservative work outfit didn't exactly scream easy money or good fashion taste. The spacious and airy showroom oozed opulence, what with its immaculately gleaming models, polished floor, casual seating area complete with tasteful magazines arranged in a fan on the coffee table and a complicated-looking coffee machine. I caught the strains of muted classical music in the background.

I started to browse around the display of cars, even though I was aware that the second-hand ones in my price range would be outside and round the back, out of sight from the main road. I wouldn't call myself a car enthusiast, but you couldn't help but admire the engineering skill that went into the design of these machines. Out of the corner of my eye I could see I was being approached by a salesman. This guy was about my age and stature, but he was better turned out and better looking than me. He was definitely not your sleazy stereotype in a cheap suit. He ambled over and gave me his best professional smile.

'Hi there,' he said. 'Anything take your eye this afternoon?'

'Well, although I've started looking in here what I'm really interested in is something a few years older. You know, a bit less pricey.' I cursed as I heard my own nervous giggle. Get a grip, I told myself. He couldn't afford one of these either.

'Yeah, I know what you mean. If we won the Lottery, eh? Let's go outside. We've got loads more cars there.'

It's true to say that I don't trust salesmen in general. Does anybody? Years ago on my degree course I did a project on the psychology of selling and marketing, and it opened my eyes to how you can be influenced without realising it. The empathy, the friendly chit chat, the body language, all work on you in subtle ways to persuade you into parting with your money. Not that any of this is rocket science, but it's surprising how susceptible even the most aware of us are to clever marketing techniques.

To give him his due, this bloke was good at his job. He was casual, knowledgeable and not too flashy or pushy. He asked what sort of car I was looking for, and I told him I fancied a convertible. He congratulated me on a good choice and gave me all the spiel about how nowadays soft tops on convertibles don't rattle like they used to and are more insulating. Neither of those things had occurred to me but I nodded sagely anyway. He nonchalantly enquired about my price range and, having done a bit of homework beforehand on what was realistic, I told him around twelve to sixteen thousand. Watching him carefully, I added casually that it would be a cash sale, and I was rewarded by catching the responding gleam in his eyes. Now it had become serious - I wasn't just one of your daydreamers getting off on looking at glamorous motors.

Jason – as his name badge told me – guided me towards a Z series roadster. I asked him what Z stood for, and I was impressed that it didn't catch him out: it stood for *Zukunft*, which is German for future, he told me. Straightaway I knew this wasn't going to be my car. It was a two-seater, all thrusting bonnet and no back, which I thought seemed out of proportion. Basically, it was a penis car. You didn't have to be a psychotherapist to realise that. So I politely let Jason know that I was thinking about something that didn't scream boy racer.

'Gotcha,' he said. 'I think our 4 series might be right up your street. We've got one in the showroom, and a couple more out here. Let's see what you think of this beauty.' Yes, the car he showed me was more up my street, but the price tag, at two thousand above my ceiling, wasn't. Jason quickly realised he'd over-pitched it and we went to what he told me was a 3 series model. The price was right, at just below 14k. I opened the door and peered in, trying to imagine myself in the driving seat. Correctly reading my thoughts, Jason said, 'We could go for a test drive, if you like.'

So he sent me off to relax with a cup of coffee while he fixed things up.

*

Why was I even contemplating buying an expensive sports car? There were two parts to the answer really. The first one, I had to admit to myself, was that I led a sensible, steady life. I did my best at work, honoured my commitments, looked after my health, blah blah blah. But when did sensible topple over into boring? When was I ever reckless or broke the rules or did something stupid just for the hell of it? About the only thing that came close to that was splitting up with Lisa, which was nothing to be proud of. I suppose I also wanted people to like and admire me – the usual human desire. I was beguiled by the idea that people would look at me driving this car and say, "hey… here's a guy who's not afraid to live life on the edge". Or words to that effect. I pictured Cora and I driving along, the wind blowing through her asymmetric hair as she sat relaxed and laughing with delight in the passenger seat while I drove her out for lunch at a countryside inn. Then there was Nathan. I would be sure to go up in his estimation if I picked him up from school in a BMW convertible. Also, looking at it practically, there would be no better time to trade in my car than the present, since I'd got brand new brakes, tyres and MOT.

Of course, there were bound to be downsides. I didn't know what the fuel economy would be like, but I could guess. You couldn't exactly say that this car was an environmentally-friendly choice. I could feel Stacey's sorrowful disapproval already. But, I reasoned, I wouldn't be using it very often. No commuting in it, for example. It wasn't difficult to talk my conscience down.

I considered seeking opinions from other people. Who? I had plenty of friends in the cycle club, but I could just imagine the reaction from some of them. They were a nice bunch, but the purists among them were of the firm view "two wheels good, four wheels bad" so they were the last people who would say what I wanted to hear. I had a few other friends locally, plus several university friends and those from back home with whom I'd kept in touch, even if it was mostly on Facebook nowadays. Most of them were married with families now, and several divorced like me. The family ones probably chose 4x4s to ferry their kids and dogs round rather than sports cars, which were usually the province of trendy single blokes. Trendy single blokes like me?

The second part of the answer as to why I could contemplate buying a sports car was simply this: I had the money. It had sat in a savings account for two years now since my grandfather died and left me £30,000 in his will. What was I going to do with the money otherwise? The obvious answer was to pay some off my mortgage, but I was managing OK, and we come back to the whole sensible and boring thing. I suppose one day I might want to trade up the flat for a house. With Cora? I couldn't see that being any time soon. We both liked our own space.

Dear old Grandad. He'd managed to clock up ninety years before we had to move him out of his own house to a nursing home. And then, mercifully in my view, he only lasted a few months. I managed to see him a few times, and I could tell that he never really allowed himself to settle into that place, despite all the care and kindness that surrounded him. At the end, I think he gave up. I hadn't known anything about the legacy until after he died. He also left money to his two other grandsons, my cousins. But I'm fairly certain that he left the major part to me.

We had a special bond, Grandad and I. I was his surrogate son.

I was fourteen when my Dad died after a heart attack. The same age as Nathan is now, in fact. A lot of my memory is pretty hazy regarding that period of my life, but what I do remember is how my grandparents rallied round when my mother was struggling just to get herself up in the morning. I ended up spending a lot of time at my grandparents' house, which was ramshackle and untidy, with dogs on the chairs and smells of hearty dinners cooking. We talked about anything and everything, including what my Dad was like when he was young. Sometimes we cried together too, but less and less as the months went by. All this was in contrast to the atmosphere at home, where Mum veered between bouts of incapacitating depression and times when she would be dolled up and going out to nightclubs, frantically enjoying herself. Of course, I understand it all much more now. A few years later Mum met and married someone else. He's OK, my stepdad. We all keep in touch.

I suppose my teenage background had a lot to do with my choice of psychology to study for my degree. I wanted to know about people's minds and their motivations, and how to help them. Then probably my own experiences of death influenced me and so I gravitated towards bereavement as a specialist area. Grandad always showed a keen interest in what I did, and he was staunchly supportive of my choices. As I said, he was like a replacement dad. Even when my marriage broke up he was on my side when few other people were. "If you know it's not right, then you're better off leaving now rather than putting up with years of misery," he said.

I wish I'd seen more of him in the last ten years. But life gets in the way. I wonder what he would have said about this sports car? I think he would have said, "Simon, I gave you that money to enjoy. If this is what you want, then do it. Life's short, and you're a long time dead."

*

102

'All you have to do is simply press that button,' said Jason. From my side in the driver's seat I duly did what I was told. The mechanism hummed into life, the hood sedately purred over my head, gradually letting in the cloudy sky. I turned round to watch the hood discreetly disappear into its secret compartment behind the back seats. Honestly, the whole operation took just seconds and it was whisper-quiet. We hadn't even driven out of the car park and I was impressed.

I drove carefully – not too sedately I hope – towards the bypass where I could open her up. I wasn't going to admit it to Jason, but this was the first time I'd actually been in a convertible. You'd think it would be draughty, but having the windows up stopped the side wind. All you felt was hair-ruffling breeze and an intoxicating sense of fresh air and freedom. Ironically, not unlike being on the bike, in some ways. The car handled beautifully too. Jason chatted affably, although I'm sure all the time he was doing his job by monitoring my reactions. He told me he and his wife had the very same car, and that she called it 'the most expensive hair dryer in the world'. We pulled up at traffic lights on the way back, and two girls waiting to cross the road, all short skirts and long hair, were definitely checking us out. Or that might have been wishful thinking on my part.

Back at the showrooms, I reluctantly slid myself out of the car. A new world of pleasure and decadence had opened up at my feet. That car had my name on it. Later, I knew I'd do my usual self-analysis on my reactions. But for now, I had to keep my wits about me to get the best trade-in on my old Honda - already consigned to the past in my mind. After some consultation between Jason his line manager, the deal was struck and I paid the deposit. We shook hands and grinned at each other. I don't know how many sales Jason typically made in a day, but I imagined him going home to his wife and bragging to her about how he clinched a sale with this boring looking guy and so earned a hefty bonus. I hoped so, anyway. I bet he got sex that night.

My step was light as I stuffed the paperwork into my pocket and pulled out my phone. The first thing I did was to message Nathan, away in the caravan with Lisa and Joe. *Hey, mate. You'll never guess what I've just bought. Show you when you get home. You'll like it. Dad.*

Chapter 12

I'd got my head together this time. Whether or not it was a good idea for me to be working with Fleur again, the die was now cast. So I planned to get on with it and conduct the session in my normal professional manner, which was second nature to me, and to be extra vigilant about maintaining my boundaries. It helped that today there wouldn't be the shock of Fleur's shorn hair to throw me off balance.

We settled into the session. Usually I can ascertain a client's mood within the first few minutes, but today I seemed to be getting mixed messages from Fleur. I picked up that she had a sort of subdued animation about her, coupled with an underlying tension. Maybe I was over-analysing. We exchanged the usual opening pleasantries, and I asked her how she'd been since we had met the previous week.

'OK,' she said. I noted that she hadn't sat back in her seat. 'I did what you told me. About the house. I've really been trying to make friends with it. After all, I've burned my bridges, like you said, so I may as well get to like it.'

I was gratified that she had taken my advice on board, and I invited her to tell me about it.

'It's a modern house, five years old. Its newness was one of the things that had put me off. Our house, Michael and mine's, was about fifty years old – ten times as old –so it had a nice mature feel to it. This one is a modern link house, and mine is in the middle of the row. It seems so small after my last one. Oh, I'm supposed to be telling you all the positive things!' She put her hands up to her face in dismay.

'That's OK. Tell me about your new home in any way it comes out.'

'Well, it's compact, but probably just the right size for one person. I've got two bedrooms, so I will be able to have visitors to stay. The kitchen is well equipped and there is room for a dining table in the living room, which I like. I can park my car on the hardstanding at the front and there's a tiny garden at the back with a few shrubs and flowers. Back inside it's got a surprising amount of cupboard space. You could call it a cosy house. I expect it will be nice and warm in the winter.' She nodded and sat back in her seat. My heart went out to her, how she was valiantly putting a positive spin on the challenges she was finding in her new home. She sounded as if she were reading from an estate agent's brochure.

'Oh, and I've made a point of meeting my next-door neighbours. I went round and introduced myself. They're really nice. One is a school teacher, and on the other side is a young couple. And they're quiet! That was a relief, because our houses are joined. You can hear the telly in the background, but that's about it. No loud music, or thumping around. If you hear voices, you can't tell what they're saying. It's quite reassuring, actually, knowing that they're there.'

'You've done really well, Fleur. It's not easy settling into a new home on your own. You're doing a great job.'

She beamed with pleasure at my praise. 'Thank you. I'm really trying to be positive.' I thought how attractive she was when her features lit up like that. I was getting used to the new short-haired Fleur. And today she had reverted to the mid-length floral skirt and loose blouse that I associated with her.

She continued telling me about her new environment. I let her run on, enjoying watching her in this vibrant mood, while at the same time I was assessing when would be an appropriate juncture to introduce the topic of the strong reaction that she had had to seeing the person who looked like Michael. My own theory, as I had mentioned to her last week, was that this reaction went hand-in-hand with her initial instability in her new home. If that were the case, then now that she was feeling more settled, the reactivation trauma over the sighting incident should similarly have subsided.

Eventually, after telling me about the birds that she was

coaxing into her little garden, her enthusiastic descriptions petered out. 'Thank you for sharing all that,' I said. 'I'm delighted that you have had the courage to respond to the challenge. Now, perhaps we could get back to...'

Before I could finish the sentence, she interrupted me. 'My life has certainly changed and I've made a lot of progress since I had those sessions with you last year. Since we met last week I've been going over how much I've moved on. It's only looking back that I realise how far I've come.'

I went along with the rather breathless diversion she had introduced and took my cue. 'Would you like to pick out anything in particular from these last months to tell me about?' I said.

Straightaway she said, 'Three months ago I registered on a dating site. My divorced friend and I did it together.' She told me which site it was and how it operated.

An unwelcome thought of Kai and his dating experiences slid into my mind. I suppressed it quickly, along with an uncomfortable twinge about what might be coming next. However, I nodded encouragingly and waited for her to tell me more.

'I was really nervous about it. My friend persuaded me that it was time to "get back out there", as she put it. She said it would be OK as long as we chose a reputable site. I didn't put on my profile that I had been widowed. Well, you wouldn't, would you? Although I saw that some men had put that. Apparently you're also not supposed to advertise that you own your house outright, because it can attract the wrong sort of attention if they think you're well off. Oh, and you have to give yourself an alias, a username, rather than broadcast your real name. Mine was "hummingbird".

'Almost as soon as my profile went up three men got in touch with me. Three! Well, I studied their profiles, and after being egged on by my friend I got in touch with one. We had some conversations online, and I found out a few basic things about him – nothing I didn't like or that freaked me out. So we fixed up a date.'

She seemed hesitant at this point about saying more, so I asked how the date went.

'Not very well. Oh, he was personable enough, but we couldn't seem to find any common ground. I wondered what on earth I was doing there. I could never in a million years imagine kissing him, let alone anything else. On his photograph he'd appeared quite handsome but…', she leaned in confidentially, 'He had bad teeth. And the worst thing was, he asked me if I was divorced, like he was. When I told him that my husband had died, he didn't know where to put himself, or how to respond. It was so embarrassing. Needless to say, we didn't arrange another date.'

'What do you feel about that experience now?'

She shrugged. 'Everyone seems to say it's par for the course. For every nice guy that you might meet, there are several that you don't hit it off with. My friend is finding it just the same.'

I must say I was quite glad about the outcome of Fleur's date. A relationship was a complication she didn't need at the moment. 'Taking the step of starting to see other men after your spouse has died is tricky,' I said. 'You need to have got to the stage where you are emotionally robust enough. What are your thoughts now about the dating site?'

I was quite surprised when she answered that she had been on dates with two other men. 'This time they were ones whom I myself had selected, rather than waiting for someone to get in touch with me. I went through all the photographs carefully to find any that looked a bit like Michael. And then I read their profiles to see if there were any who seemed similar to him.'

Whoa. This rang alarm bells. 'Why did you do that, Fleur?'

'As I said, to see if there was anybody like Michael.' She seemed puzzled by the question. 'Anyway, there were two I picked out. But when I came to meet them face to face, neither of them resembled Michael at all. These photos can be so misleading. I found they weren't like him in manner, either. It was all rather disappointing. That happened before I moved house, and I haven't had the time or inclination to bother since.'

'Let me clarify what I think I've just heard from you. Your first date, with someone who was not of your choosing, was not successful and left you feeling emotionally exposed. Therefore you reasoned that someone who reminded you of Michael might give you more security. Then you discovered that didn't work out in practice. Even though two people can have superficial characteristics or interests in common, each individual person is unique and needs to be treated as such.'

She frowned and shifted in her seat 'I don't know,' she said. I mentally rehearsed what I would write in her case notes after the session. *Client exhibited unrealistic expectations…*

I decided, given her discomfort, there was probably no benefit at present in trying to explore her Michael-centred approach to the dating website. It would be better to leave it until next session when she would have had time to think it through. Besides which, we had spent a fair bit of this session talking about her new home. This was fruitful, I judged, because of her progress and positivity, but now time was getting on and we needed to get back to Fleur's response to the episode of the man in the park. After all, this incident was why she had elected to come back for more counselling.

'By the way,' she said, 'I won't be able to come in for the next two weeks There are loads of people off work taking annual leave, so it would be difficult for me to take an afternoon off. I'll be back in the following week, though.'

I recognised this as her steer to change the subject. 'That's fine,' I said. 'We'll make sure on your way out that Lucy has it in the calendar.' She seemed to be looking more receptive again, so I said, 'Could we get back to what we were discussing last week about the man you saw who so strongly reminded you of Michael? You were quite disturbed by that encounter. How do you feel about it now?'

My expectation was that, coupled with the strides forward she had made in befriending her new personal environment, she would have been able to put the incident behind her. In other words, my professional assessment of the situation would have been vindicated. I couldn't have been more wrong.

'I've seen him in the park again,' she said. 'I've been going there every day and on Sunday he was there.' I could hear the supressed excitement in her voice.

I kept my features neutral and encouraging. 'Do you mean that you were going to the park deliberately to see if this man turned up, or were you just going for a walk?'

She looked defensive. 'The park's a nice place for exercise,' she said.

I didn't ask her to disambiguate. 'Did you speak to him?'

She shook her head. 'No. He was sitting at a table outside the café having coffee with an older couple, so I didn't like to intrude. He had the dog with him. It was the dog I noticed first.'

Oh, Fleur. I was gathering my response when she said, 'I was nervous about going up to him. You see, I don't know what he'd think about my hair being cut off.'

*

I'll pick you up at midday, with a picnic. I've got a surprise for you! Xxx.

It was my turn to get my own back by sending Cora a cryptic message, like she had sent to me. Only there's no comparison between the surprise being a BMW convertible and it being a new haircut, albeit a geometrical one, so I figure I won hands down. I was looking forward to telling her that. In the nicest possible way, of course. And I couldn't wait to see her face when I showed her the surprise.

I was keeping my eye on the weather forecast for Bank Holiday Monday, and it seemed we were in luck. The day dawned bright and fairly sunny, with a chance of thundery showers later in the day, the Met office said. Well, that was good enough for me. If there's one thing that would be almost as bad as having a picnic in the rain, it would be driving a convertible around in the rain with the hood up. Not that the car wasn't weatherproof, I assume (note-to-self to confirm its integrity during the next rainy period), but you miss the whole point if you drive with the roof up. Then it's just a car.

I'd popped into my local Waitrose that morning and bought the components for a slap-up picnic, a real gourmet job, if I say so myself. Smoked salmon, salads, cheeseboard, savouries, rolls, fruit and fancy cakes plus a bottle of wine, of which I would allow myself one glass. I also realised that I didn't have a cool box, a rug to sit on, or any picnicware, so I'd had to equip myself with all that too. This was going to be a serious feast. Not bad for a bloke.

Cora answered her door to me looking as fresh as ever, in white jeans, sandals, a floppy hat and a bright pink T-shirt that outlined her breasts nicely. I kissed her and complimented her on how nice she looked. We went into her lounge, which had canvases stacked everywhere.

'Ready for the big day, eh?' I said, indicating the stacks of canvases which seemed to be leaning against every available vertical surface in the room.

'Getting there,' she said. 'Only twelve days to go now. I've got to make some final choices from this lot, depending on how they look when they're in the hall.' We surveyed the piles.

'By the way,' she said, 'Were you able to put a flyer up at work?' I assured her that a colourful poster was adorning the notice board for clients to see when they came in. 'What with targeting local libraries, Facebook, other social media and now the local press on board, I think I've done what I can with publicity,' she said.

She offered me coffee but I said I'd rather we got going for our picnic. I eyed her flimsy T-shirt and suggested that she bring something a bit warmer to wear on top. When she looked puzzled, I said it was connected with the surprise. I thought that would give the game away, but it seemed not. Her eyes widened in astonishment when we went outside and I led her up to the BMW and made a big show of opening the passenger door with a flourish. Out of the corner of my eye I saw a couple of young kids with bikes watching open-mouthed from the other side of the street.

'Well, this is posh,' she said as she climbed into the seat, somewhat gingerly I thought. 'When you said to take an extra top, I thought we were going on a boat trip. A convertible car didn't occur to me. Have you hired it for the day?'

I climbed into the driving seat beside her and started the engine with an unnecessary roar. 'Nope.' I was enjoying this. 'It's all mine. Buckle up, sweetheart.'

After removing her hat before the breeze did it for her, she floundered for words. 'Goodness... I don't know what to say... I had no idea you were going to buy a car like this. It must have been terribly expensive.'

'I'll tell you all about it when we get there. You just sit back and enjoy the ride. I thought we'd go to Virginia Water.' We headed south for the short time that it took and swung into the carpark. I found myself wishing that I'd chosen somewhere further away to show the car off more. It was a perfect day for it.

'What do you think of this,' I said. 'A one finger job.' I pressed the button and the hood glided almost noiselessly over our heads and latched neatly into place. It still delighted me. Cora had pulled her comb out of her bag and was tidying her hair. Not that it was particularly messed up, as far as I could tell. 'Very slick,' she said. The whole experience seemed to be overwhelming her.

I gathered up the picnic accoutrements from the boot and we set off around the lake. It was quite busy today, being a Bank Holiday with decent weather. Dogs bounded around, toddlers shrieked and families grouped on picnic rugs. While we walked I filled Cora in on how Kai had first put the idea of the car into my mind, how I had gone to the showroom just to have a look, and how I'd decided there and then to go for it. 'As you know, I'm not usually an impulsive person, but this car seemed to have my name on it,' I said.

'Well, it's a very nice car,' she said. 'You seem thrilled with it, and that's the main thing.'

A very nice car? *Nice?* I bit back my irritation. Talk about "damning with faint praise". And she sounded patronising, as if she were talking to a child. We walked on in silence while I made an effort to subdue my petulance. She asked where we were going to have the picnic and I shrugged and said why didn't she choose somewhere. She settled on what she considered was a good spot, which was a little way back from the lake, under some trees. I spread the new rug with a flourish and started to unpack the goodies. This time her response was a bit more like it. The wine and various platters were met with exclamations of astonishment and she complimented me on putting together such a fabulous lunch. An inspired lunch, she said.

I felt somewhat mollified by the success of the picnic. After all, I had put a lot of thought into it. I suspected that Cora was making a special effort in order to make up for her lukewarm response to my beautiful new car. My "very nice car".

'This picnic was a lovely idea of yours,' she said. 'Thank you for putting it together.' She leaned over and kissed me on the cheek. 'You're very welcome,' I said. She did look particularly pretty sitting there in the shade of the tree, her plastic wine glass dangling in her hand and her lips pink like her T-shirt. I told her so and was rewarded by another kiss. I decided to let the whole car thing go. It was a glorious day; why spoil it?

'I was surprised when you suggested we went out today,' she said. 'Often you spend time with Nathan on a Saturday.'

'They're away on holiday. But next Saturday I'm going to see them, before the boys go back to school.' I recognised and appreciated her concession in mentioning Nathan, which was a rare thing for her. I wondered briefly how they were all getting on in the caravan. Nathan was probably bored out of his skull and Joe might well be playing up. Poor old Lisa.

I pulled my thoughts back to the woman sitting on the rug with me. 'So it's not long now to the exhibition,' I said. 'A week on Saturday?'

'Mmm. I'm starting to get nervous.'

'That's only natural. But lots of people say how good your work is, and you've put so much preparation in. Do you want me to help on the day?' I hoped she hadn't noticed the slight hesitation before my question.

'No, I think I've got it covered. The drinks and canapes are on order. A few of my students are coming in the afternoon with a van to do the transporting and to help me set up. Then it's a five-thirty start. You'll be there nice and early, won't you?'

'I wouldn't miss it.' I hoped I sounded sincere. I really did want the exhibition to be a success for her, but I had to admit that I wasn't looking forward to it. Having to stand around and hobnob with arty types when I didn't have a clue what I was talking about left me feeling distinctly insecure. I could just imagine their eyebrows shooting up with barely concealed disbelief when they asked me how I knew Cora and I had to reveal I was her boyfriend. But I mustn't let her down.

'Whew, I should stop drinking now. I'm having too much for a lunchtime. You normally drink half the bottle, that's the trouble.' Cora drained what was left in her glass and lay down with her head on my lap.

'Shall we stay in and watch a film tonight and get a takeaway?' she said. 'After this lunch I feel too lazy to want to go out.'

'If that's what you prefer. I'm happy to stay in.'

She put her hand on my thigh, just above my knee. 'We could also start talking about holiday possibilities.'

That was a turn up. I'd more or less given up on the topic. 'If you like,' I said. I thought it was best not to sound too

114

enthusiastic.

Her fingers moved ever so slightly on my thigh. 'I fancy going somewhere quite hot, but where we could do some sightseeing as well as lolling in the sun. I'd still rather do the actual booking after the exhibition, though. And that way we'll get a last-minute bargain, if we're not too fussy where we go.'

'Any ideas?'

'Well, Greece is good if we're thinking about Europe. Or then there's somewhere like Mexico if we want to go long haul.'

So it seemed it was game on after all. It had gone from perhaps not happening at all to possibly going half-way round the world. I trailed my fingers over her forehead and hair. 'OK. We can chat later,' was all I risked saying at this stage.

I looked out at the pleasant summer scene of water, trees and lazing people. Cora's head had gone heavy on my lap and I saw she had dozed off, her breathing even and shallow. Idle thoughts of relaxing like this in some exotic location trickled through my head. I wondered if there were hummingbirds in Mexico.

*

I had rarely felt more furtive than I did when I was hunched over my laptop with a selection of pretty girls smiling out at me from the screen. Although I know it's not the same thing, it took me right back to my teenage years and the well-thumbed magazines, swapped around between my mates and me, that I kept hidden under my bed. I don't think my Mum would have been very bothered if she'd come across them. She always had other things on her mind.

It's not that I'm against dating websites and apps. They're as good a way as any to meet people. It's just that I've never found the need. And, I suppose, I have a lingering prejudice that there's something distasteful about them, like porn. Yet look at Kai. Tinder has turned out to have given him a new lease of life. I don't imagine that Tinder is anything like the glossy and sophisticated set up that I was presented with on my laptop. According to Kai, Tinder is swipe the screen and off you go, whereas here there was a sequence of steps that seemed quite complex to me. And, of course, I couldn't ask Kai for advice. No one, but no-one, must know about this. This little undertaking was my guilty secret, to be carried out alone in my flat late at night.

I could have simply walked away. I could have logged off, watched half an hour of mindless TV, sent a night-night text to Cora, cleaned my teeth and fallen into bed. In fact, I did start that process. I was sprawled on the sofa watching the antics on the screen with glazed eyes when I realised I hadn't taken anything in for the last ten minutes. So there I was again, this time with my credit card in my hand punching in the numbers which would open the magic door. I discovered that I didn't need to set up a profile of my own to search through the abundance of available women who were hoping to meet their dream man. Or just someone halfway decent to go out with.

As I had hoped, there was a search facility, and I found her straight away. Hummingbird. I wondered why Fleur had chosen that username, and yet it suited her perfectly: a tiny bird that was pretty and delicate and elusive. It was a good photograph, and it did her justice. She was smiling only a little, with her head slightly lowered, which gave an understated effect. It spoke of enigma and gentle depths. No wonder there were men who wanted to meet her.

After I had stopped gazing at her photo I read her detailed profile, and then read it again. It was brimming with little nuggets of information, giving me access to things we hadn't had reason to touch upon in our sessions together and fleshing her out more as a person. She had obviously given considerable thought as to how best to present herself and what facts to include. I didn't know, for instance, that she loves animals and had a pet dog when she was a child. She is also interested in birds and is a member of the RSPB. One of her favourite foods is strawberries, her favourite colour is blue and she reads the Independent. She hates loud noises. So many things I hadn't known. As her therapist, it gave me more insight into her character and background. So you could look upon it as research rather than an unpardonable breach of trust and invasion of her privacy.

I don't know what he'd think about my hair being cut off... I thought back to the closing minutes of my last session with her, when she was telling me how she chose not to approach 'Michael' in the cafe. A golden rule in my job is, at a delicate juncture when you can't judge the best way to respond, play for time. Say nothing. Let the ball stay in the client's court and maybe they will tell you more without you having to lead them. So that's what I did. The seconds had ticked by. She had averted her face from me, making it hard to gauge her expression. Defiant? Sad? Confused? All of them? Eventually I had to break the silence.

'Is this a game, Fleur?'

'I don't know,' she had said, after a long silence.

We left it there. We were almost out of time, but also she needed some space to reflect. I said we would return to this next time.

I stared again at her photo on screen. What's going on in your head, hummingbird? But there were no immediate answers and it was getting late. I went back to the home screen of the dating site, thinking what a polished script Fleur had put together. Was this usual, or was hers better than the norm? Before I went to bed I thought I would have a quick glance at some of the others. There were the smiling faces again. I clicked on a few. Some had desperate big grins, lacking the subtlety inherent to Fleur's photo. A few didn't have a photo at all, and some had rather sparse, clumsy profiles. Out of curiosity, I looked to see if the men's were any better. They weren't. And in fact, more of them didn't have a photo than in the women's section. So what was to stop someone making up a bogus profile, omitting a photo, and making contact with someone else on the site?

117

Chapter 13

'Fuck me! is it yours, Dad?' Normally I wouldn't encourage language like that from Nathan – in fact it might be the only time he'd ever sworn freely in front of me – but in the circumstances he was excused. Whereas Cora's reaction to my new car had been polite but tepid, which really I should have predicted, Nathan's couldn't have been more different. I don't remember when I'd seen him more excited, even counting recently when I said he could go to France.

I stood aside with shy pride while he walked round the car admiring it from all angles, asking questions about its top speed and acceleration. I hadn't known he was so interested in cars, but then, he's a fourteen-year-old boy. He asked if he could sit in the driving seat, where he lovingly ran his hands over the steering wheel and hefted the gear lever. Thrusting his phone at me, he asked me to take a picture of him and the whole car. I obliged. I thought of asking him to swap round and take one of me and the car, but on the other hand I was more than gratified with his reaction, so I didn't bother. I could see this heralding a new era in father-son bonding. I watched, somewhat amused, while he punched the screen and I knew that within seconds the picture of my car would be doing the rounds all over Instagram or whatever social media platform was popular with the kids now.

'So are you ready to go for a road trip? Are you free all day?' I'd already given him advance warning that I'd got something planned that could take several hours. Today the weather forecast promised us a hot sunny day with no chance of rain. There was no mention of thundery showers, as there had been last Monday. On the way back to Cora's the sky had darkened ominously and a few drops of rain had squeezed out onto us. Cora had insisted that I pull over and put the hood up, even though it wasn't much of a sprinkling.

Nathan was just giving his eager approval to the road-trip

plan when we were joined by Joe.

'I saw you through the window.' He announced this in his solemn, Joe-like way. He inspected the car with wide eyed interest. 'Is it your car?' he said.

'It is.' I squatted down beside him. 'Would you like to sit inside it?' From the driving seat he informed me that he liked cars that didn't have a top. I thought with a guilty pang that I was colluding with both the boys to embrace something that was definitely un-green, whereas what I really should be instilling in them was a respect for the environment. But, having bought the car, that would be hypocritical. Still, I'd salve my conscience later by mentioning that I was intending to use the car sparingly and that motoring on the whole was bad for the planet. Meanwhile, I intended to enjoy a day with my son.

'Where are we going?' said Nathan. I waved my hand to indicate the open road. 'We've got a full tank of petrol. Any ideas?'

'How about Brighton?'

Brighton? All the way to the south coast? That certainly was a road trip alright. But I realised I would look pretty feeble if I raised objections.

Nathan was one step ahead of me and was already consulting Google Maps. 'One hour twenty-five minutes. Perfect.'

Well, why not? There was never going to be a nicer day to investigate the car's quirks and to put it through its paces. I was just thinking this when Lisa showed up, her hair wrapped in a towel turban, grinning all over her face. 'I wondered where everybody was. Oh my God, Simon, what a fantastic car!' I briefly went over the spiel about how I had come to be the proud owner of a BMW, and that I had dear old Grandad to thank for it.

Lisa had taken the towel off her head and was rubbing her damp hair. 'Do you remember,' she said to me, 'Years ago when we took it in turns to pose by a sports car and took each other's photo, then the owner came running out of the restaurant and shooed us off?' Actually I had completely forgotten about that episode, but as soon as she said it the memory came flooding back, as memories can. I recalled how we had escaped around the corner and couldn't stop laughing. Those were the days.

'We're going on a trip to Brighton,' said Nathan. 'I'll just pick up my jacket then I'm good to go.'

At this Joe pricked up his ears. 'I want to go for a ride in the car too,' he said.

I tried to explain. Lisa tried to explain. Nathan and I were going on a special day out, we told him. I promised Joe I would take him out in the car soon. Lisa also made it clear that she wouldn't be happy about Joe sitting in the back on his own with the roof down. Now, if he'd had a tantrum while all this was going on, I might have been able to resist him. But he just looked so crestfallen and sad, poor little chap. I took a deep breath and asked, with some trepidation, would Nathan be prepared to sit in the back with Joe? Bad move.

'You've got to be joking,' said Nathan. 'That totally sucks. What do you think I am, a babysitter?'

'Don't talk to your Dad like that.'

'He didn't say anything about Joe coming!'

I could feel the day slipping away from me. 'Let's all calm down, shall we?' I said. Three unhappy faces confronted me, not made any less so by my suggestion. Then I had an idea and clutched at it. 'Lisa, are you doing anything today that you couldn't change? I'm thinking, how about if we all go?'

Silence. Then Lisa said. 'I was going to go shopping, but that's all. Are you really sure about this?'

I hesitated, then for the second time in half an hour I thought, why not. About the only time we went out all together was on the boys' birthdays. 'Yes, I'm sure. A day out for us all in Brighton will be fun.' Nathan was still looking sulky so I said, 'Come on, Nath. Be the big person here. Tell you what, I'll finish work early one day soon and come and pick you up from school.

Deal?'

So it was settled. Lisa said could I wait while she dried her hair. 'Why bother?' I said. 'You've got the most expensive hairdryer in the world right here.'

*

When I thought of that trip to Brighton afterwards, it stood out in my mind as a golden day. On the drive down south Joe and Lisa cheered and waved to other motorists in their vehicles while Nathan tried to ignore his family and look cool in his shades. We found ourselves a place to park a little way out of the city and sauntered in, all in a holiday mood. The general consensus was that we should head for the seafront to buy chips and ice cream, which seemed as good a plan as any. When I had eaten my breakfast earlier today I had no notion that I would end up just a few hours later at the seaside. The day seemed surreal; it was like a dream where I was transported back to the days of my childhood holidays, complete with a giant pier and the endless sea. And yet Lisa, Nathan and Joe were here too.

I could see why Nathan had suggested coming to Brighton. It was brash, noisy, colourful, alive, vibrant, pulsating, with a larger-than-life vibe about it that left other seaside towns behind by a mile. Definitely a young person's place. We got our cans of drink to go with our chips and sat down on the pebbly beach, wriggling around to get comfy on the stones, along with dozens of other people also out to enjoy the sunshine. We sat in a row and picked up the fat golden chips with our fingers, biting at them gingerly because they were hot and fresh. Just like a normal family, in fact.

To our left the pier jutted out to sea, a monster construction if ever there was one. I expected Joe, and probably Nathan, to be clamouring to taste the garish funfair delights that were on the pier, which might have happened had they not clapped eyes on the tower stuck up into the sky on our right. This, I was informed by Nathan, was the new British Airways i360 tower. I could best describe it as a tall – and I mean colossal – pole pointing upwards with a doughnut-shaped glass pod encircling it. After looking at it for a while you could see that the pod moved and was presumably full of people. At present it was gliding back down to earth. What an audacious piece of engineering.

It turned out that one of Nathan's mates had gone up in this thing – a 'flight', it's called – and had raved about it. 'If we'd known we could have booked,' I said. 'As it is, they're probably full.'

Nathan was consulting his phone. 'We're in luck. They have spaces on a flight later this afternoon.'

'Are we going up into the sky?' said Joe.

'I don't think so,' said Lisa. 'We can have just as much fun playing here on the pebbles. We can go down to the sea and get our feet wet.' She didn't do a bad job of keeping the wistfulness out of her voice.

'Shall I book this or not? Only we shouldn't wait around or it'll be gone.'

'Nathan, don't pressurise your Dad. It's enough that he's brought us here without adding an expensive thing like that too.'

'Let's go for it,' I said. 'All four of us.'

The words were hardly out of my mouth before Nathan was on it. He held his hand out. 'Got your credit card?' Belatedly he added, 'Please.'

Meekly I handed it over and he did the business. I felt Lisa touch my hand. 'Is this OK?' she said. 'It's ever so expensive.'

I said, 'It's fine. Let's make today a mini holiday.' What the hell.

*

There was time for a wander round the town and ice creams, which Lisa insisted on paying for, before we headed to the 'Departure Lounge' ahead of our flight. Even though we had browsed gift stalls and little shops, the boys wisely didn't ask for

123

anything else. While we were gathered in the Departure Lounge there was a video you could view about how the tower had been constructed. There was a definite sense of supressed anticipation as we waited, our eyes on the screen with its images of mighty cranes hoisting girders aloft. 'When are we going up into the sky?' said Joe. 'Soon,' said Lisa.

We watched, fascinated, as the cabin whispered down the pole to ground level. Passengers processed out to the other side, and we waited for our turn. I noticed that Joe didn't demur about having his hand held by Lisa while we shuffled in, nor was he bothered by the temporary crush of people. Once in – aboard, I should say – you could walk freely around the entire circle of the glass pod. The excitement mounted as we lifted off and started to ascend the pole. People, traffic, buildings, started to recede as we climbed higher. Joe was transfixed, his nose almost glued to the glass. Lisa virtually had to prise him away to encourage him to move from the city view to look at the coast and sea. I realised with something of a shock that Joe had never been in an aeroplane. Not yet, anyway.

There was no problem with Nathan moving around to take in all the aspects. I looked for him and found him elbowing his way through people at the glass and then flitting to a new vantage point and doing the same again. I caught up with him and we stood together silently watching the glorious sprawl of the city gradually opening up below us, backed by the hills of the South Downs in the distance. Overlaid on the view was the long finger of the shadow made by the tower, dwarfing all the other shadows. You could actually see the pod's shadow moving gently on its journey upwards, and then downwards. I joined Lisa and Joe to point out the shadow to them. I wasn't sure if Joe took it in, but he was spellbound anyway. Lisa turned to me. 'This is amazing,' she said.

I don't know which gave me more pleasure, seeing the birds' eye view or watching Nathan, Lisa and Joe watching it. Twenty-five minutes after we had started we were gliding back to earth again and things resumed their normal perspective, rendered slightly boring now. We were all rather dazed by the experience, and as we walked back to the car we were initially less chatty than might have been expected. I asked Joe what bit he liked best. I expected that he would say something about the view of all the buildings, but what he said was he liked the way the sky got all big. I wondered what impact this would have on his drawings.

Joe had been tired and getting whiny when we first got back to the car, but we plied him and ourselves with sandwiches and drink that we had bought from a convenience store and hoped that would boost his energy levels. Lisa was fussing about crumbs getting dropped onto the car's upholstery, but I said not to bother about it. I was feeling magnanimous that day, and it was a sensation to be savoured. Joe got his second wind when we were cruising along and he started waving to other motorists again.

Nathan said, 'That was a great day out, Dad. It was, like, epic.' I told him it was my pleasure, and I meant it. I added I hoped he hadn't minded too much that it was all of us, not just him and me. He answered that it was OK and grabbed the opportunity to ask if I'd meant it when I said I would pick him up from school one day. And so, after a quick mental review of my diary, we pencilled it in for Wednesday. This called for another flurry of activity with his phone. I guessed I was to expect a small crowd on Wednesday.

The drive back was a rewind of the drive out. No traffic problems, no hold-ups, desultory chatting with Nathan. I mentally did a quick tot-up of how much I'd spent during the day. After I'd recoiled in shock, I decided not to think about it again. It had been worth it, on every front.

When we pulled up at Lisa's house, she asked me if I'd like to come in for a coffee or something. I considered it, then declined. A return to the everyday would have broken the spell. I got out of the car to see them all inside. Lisa gave me a kiss on the cheek and told me it had been a brilliant day and that I'd been so generous. Nathan and I nodded to each other and briefly clasped hands as we do sometimes nowadays. Then there was the whole "now what do you say to Simon" routine with Joe. He obeyed with the expected response of "thank you, Simon", then he suddenly threw his arms around me and gave me a hug that must have lasted a whole four seconds. His head only came up to my middle, bless him. As I tentatively put my arms around him I met Lisa's look over his head, both of us wide-eyed and gobsmacked. It was almost unknown for me to get a hug from Joe.

I drove away, waving up in the air to them and saw them fade from my rear-view mirror. I headed home, parked up and went into my flat. I was about to message Cora when I remembered she was out on some girly do or other. I pictured what would be going on in Lisa's house now. Nathan would no doubt have retreated to his room and his virtual world. Joe would be going through his bedtime routine. Or did he stay up later on a Saturday? I didn't know. Did he still have a bedtime story with Lisa? I didn't know. None of that was my world.

Chapter 14

It started with me having time to kill on Saturday afternoon. I'd gone out with Nathan, taken him for a fast-food lunch and then shopped with him for new trainers. That boy was certainly shooting up. After that I dropped him off because he had an arrangement to meet his mates, and I didn't want to crash that. What was I to do with a spare couple of hours? It wasn't worth going home. So I got back into the car and pointed it to drive where it would. And, lo and behold, we were heading into the town where Fleur lived.

Well, I can drive where I like, can't I? I spotted what must be the park that she'd talked about. I saw the wrought iron gates standing open and I had a view of greenery inside as I crawled past in the Saturday afternoon shopping traffic. I turned sharp left after the park and luckily found a parking space in that street. A stretch of my legs in the park would be just the job now, even though the sky was overcast. I took the footpath that traced all around the edge of park, past benches and flowerbeds that had an end-of-summer look about them, a couple of tennis courts and the café under the canopy. I went up to it and scanned the tables. About half of them were occupied, and there was a beguiling smell of coffee hanging around the chit-chat of the small groups. It only took me perhaps ten minutes to do the circuit.

Fleur's house was to the right when you came out of the park, down the main street and then second turning on the left. I had looked up her address on file in the office. What's wrong with that? I am perfectly entitled to get the file out and look at it. Even when Lucy isn't there. And yes, I had checked the location of her house on Google maps, so I knew where it was in relation to the park. It could be useful background information to see her house, given how much she'd talked about it in our sessions. It wasn't as if I was going to knock on her door and see if she was home, was it? Now that would be crossing the line.

I turned right and walked down the street, past various outlets such as charity shops, a pub, a bank, Tesco Express, Boots and a newsagent. A typical line-up for a small town, and I mused on the facelessness of towns nowadays. I looked at the other people on the street. Were they faceless too? Not really. There were different ethnicities, ages, groups, modes of dress. I paid special attention to them all. There was a young street person sitting on the on pavement staring into space. I gave him a pound and he muttered his thanks. I checked my watch. I was in a two-hour parking slot and there was still plenty of time.

I was coming up to a greengrocer's shop. It was an old-fashioned one, like you might imagine finding in a village, with heaped trays of colourful fruit and veg outside under a green awning. I probably couldn't name all of the produce on display, but I could appreciate that it looked far more appealing there than in plastic bags in a supermarket. The shop had more character than any other of the bland establishments on the High Street. That's how my thoughts were running when suddenly she was there, a car's length or so away from me, walking out of the greengrocer's with two laden carrier bags.

We spotted each other at the same time and we both stopped short. Fleur's face was initially blank, that look that you have when you see someone out of context; you know you recognise them, but you can't place them straightaway. But only for a couple of seconds. Then she smiled and turned towards me.

'Simon! What a surprise. Whatever brings you around here?'

It was just as well that she spoke first, because I was tongue-tied. Gobsmacked. Astounded. I struggled to pull myself together and managed to say, 'Hello, Fleur. Yes, a surprise indeed. I've been doing some shopping with my son.' Not a lie, because I had been shopping with Nathan earlier. And it was only about half an hour away.

'I didn't know you had a son. I didn't even know you were married.'

'Well, why would you? In our sessions it's all about you, not me. And I'm divorced, by the way.' I hoped my speech didn't sound as unnatural to her as it did to me. I had imagined, fantasised if you like, about bumping into Fleur but I never dreamt it would actually happen. Now that it had, I couldn't quite get my head around it. One thing was clear: I must not blow it.

'Oh,' was all she said. We both hesitated, awkward. She put down the two shopping bags, which I took to be a sign that she wanted to prolong the conversation. I said the first thing that came into my head. 'This looks like a great shop. Do you get all of your fresh stuff here?'

'Most of it. I like to eat quality fruit and vegetables.'

A woman pushing a man in a wheelchair went past us with a pointed "excuse me". 'We're getting in people's way here,' I said. 'Would you like to get a cup of tea somewhere?'

I held my breath while she considered her answer. Then she said that it would be lovely and led the way to a Costa just off the main street. We exchanged pleasantries about the town and the weather while we walked. I bought tea for us both, shooting glances at her now and then while I waited in the queue.

We sat facing each other across the small table. The Costa was quite full, mainly with groups of teenagers, as you might expect on a Saturday afternoon. I watched her small hands as she poured the tea for us both. We smiled over the rims of our cups, and I met her eyes for as long as I dared. It wasn't a first internet date – not a date at all, of course - but I felt as nervous as if it were. She made the first conversational move.

'This feels a bit weird,' she said. 'But it's good to see you in a different context like this.' She frowned. 'It is OK, isn't it? I mean, within your rules?'

I didn't want to tell her the truth, that is, we were already outside the guidelines for good practice. Instead I said, 'We can treat this as an unintentional social occasion. After all, it's not as if it were planned. But we shouldn't turn it into a counselling session.'

'In that case, tell me a bit about yourself.'

So I told her about Nathan and Joe, without going into details about Joe's parentage, and about my love of cycling. I told her where I lived. I was surprised by how interested she was in it all. Or was she just being polite? We lightly passed the conversational ball back and forth until we had finished our tea. It was, I have to say, very similar to a first date. I've been on a few of those in my time.

Outside I asked her if she would like a lift to her house, because my car was only around the corner. She accepted. I offered to carry her shopping bags, like a gentleman should, but she said she could manage. She gave me directions, and I pretended not to know them. I pulled up outside the small house, one in a linked row, as she had described it a couple of sessions ago. She thanked me for the tea, then after a pause asked me if I'd like to come in and see inside. After a pause of matching length I said I would.

'I'm not sure how tidy it is,' she said, 'because I wasn't expecting company.' She hung my jacket just inside the door in the miniscule entrance hall and we went from there into the living room. It all looked tidy enough to me and I told her so. She showed me round the living room and the kitchen, almost apologising for how small it all was. I said, quite truthfully, that it was bigger than my one-bedroomed flat. And she had a garden too.

'Gosh, I never thought of that. I mean, lots of people live in small flats. Hmm. I think I've settled in here now. It's getting to feel like home.' She put out a hand and laid it against the wall, as if she were literally feeling its vibrations. There were various pictures on the wall, framed photographs and ornaments tastefully arranged on every surface, scatter cushions and rugs in abundance. Very much a feminine room, I thought.

'Look,' she said, leading me over to a cabinet and picking up one of the photographs that were displayed there. 'This is our wedding.' I took the picture from her and gazed at the standard group of parents, best man, bridesmaids and the happy couple, Fleur in the traditional long white dress. She was standing right next to me as I held the picture, so close that I could hear her breathing and inhale her clean smell.

'It's a great picture,' I said, aware that it wasn't a particularly adequate response. She handed me a second photo. 'And this is Michael a couple of years ago.' I saw a slim man who was casually dressed and wearing a hat, sitting on a patio at a table. He had brown eyes and an affable smile. 'He looks like a really nice man,' I said. She put the picture back and traced her finger over his face. 'He was,' she said. 'He was.'

She gestured at the picture. 'You see the hat that he was wearing? That's the hat he wore most of the time. I've kept it. Can I show you?' She led me back to the hall and handed me the light coloured trilby with a dark band around it that was hanging there. She'd told me about this special hat before. I held it reverently for a minute before handing it back to her. She sighed and hung it back on the hook.

'Could I see the garden?' I said. She readily agreed, and took me into the little green space, which was actually quite delightful, like a secret arbour. She became reanimated as she showed me the bird bath that she'd recently bought and reported that there were various feathered visitors already.

'Ah yes, you're interested in birds, I remember.' I could have bitten my tongue. But luckily she didn't seem to remember that she had never told me that. I'd got it from the dating website. We went back inside and she offered me more tea. When we were settled on the sofa with our cups and a plate of biscuits, I said, 'Are you content here, Fleur?'

She thought for a minute before she answered. 'Content enough. I've got used to living alone, and moving house has helped with that. I guess that's closure, isn't it? Oh, and I'll go to the park again tomorrow. I haven't seen him lately, but maybe he'll be walking his dog then because it's Sunday.'

The last thing I wanted to do was to engage with the whole

Michael look-alike thing. Today was special and I didn't want to spoil it. And anyway, we weren't having a counselling session. So I side-stepped it and said, 'I'm glad you're settling down in your new home.'

And then we just chatted for a while. I can't even properly remember what about now, but I know that it was pleasant. Eventually I said I ought to go and she brought my jacket in. My hand touched hers as she passed it to me, and I stroked her fingers lightly before I put the jacket on. It seemed totally natural, inevitable perhaps, to put my arms around her and hold her. She felt tiny, my hummingbird, almost insubstantial. I kept my hug light and gentle. Apart from putting her arms around me to return the embrace, she was passive. I moved my lips to her cheek and kissed it. Then I had to let her go and say my goodbye. We both said how nice it had been and that we would be meeting next Friday at The Willows. She waved goodbye from her doorstep. Nice. Yes, it had been nice.

I drove down the road until I was out of sight of her house, and then pulled up and turned the engine off. I stared out of the window for a few minutes, trying to reorient myself. Then it occurred to me that I had absolutely no idea what the time was. I pulled out my phone and checked. No... no... *no*, it couldn't be half past six! Oh God. There were three messages, all from Cora.

The first one said,

Hi darling, are you running late? The exhibition is all set up and it looks great. See you soon x

Then,

Simon, I'm getting worried. Just send me a text, will you?

And finally,

WHERE ARE YOU???

*

'Is it just me, or was Neville a bit weird this morning?' It was Stacey who said what we were all thinking as we trooped out of

132

the team meeting, relieved to be out of the stuffy room.

Emma agreed. 'Yes, he seemed jittery, distracted. Not his usual smooth self at all.'

'I was bracing myself for the latest news on changes to the practice, aromatherapy and all that crap, but he didn't mention it at all,' said Kai.

We four stalwarts congregated in the kitchen for what had become our customary chat, slouching about with our folders and notebooks under our arms while other attendees of the meeting were drifting off to their various responsibilities. It occurred to me, through the fog that inhabited my head that Monday morning, how fully Kai had woven himself into life at The Willows.

Neville swept out of the staff room at that point, sent us all a curt nod and strode into his office, closing the door firmly behind him. Lucy followed him out, juggling her laptop and a sheaf of papers which she dumped onto her desk. She gave us her usual generous and slightly cheeky smile – the very opposite of Neville – and said, 'There's still some coffee left in the pot if you want to finish it. But there's only three biscuits so you'll have to fight over them.'

As it happened there wasn't any negotiation called for because I didn't fancy another biscuit. More coffee was good, though.

'You're quiet today, Simon. We can usually rely on you to entertain us in the meeting with a bit of sparring between you and Neville.' This was from Emma. All three of them were looking at me, with expressions of concern mixed with curiosity on their faces, so I had to rouse myself and say something.

'Yeah, well, I didn't sleep very much last night and I've had a bit of an odd weekend, so it was as much as I could do to keep awake in there, to be honest.'

There were sympathetic mutterings all round. Emma excused herself to go and get ready for her upcoming client.

'Family problems, is it mate?' said Kai.

'No. No, nothing like that.' Cora's bewildered hurt, my lame, virtually inarticulate excuses, the stand-up row that happened yesterday, all flashed on the screen in my head yet again.

After a minute Kai shrugged. 'Well, you know where to find me if you want to offload. Right, I'm off then. I only came in this morning for that lousy meeting. What a waste of time.'

The extra coffee had helped. I had half an hour to get my act together for my next client. A woman, with unresolved bereavement issues. A woman who wasn't Fleur.

Stacey, kind little Stacey, put her hand on my arm and looked closely into my face. 'You do look a bit peaky, you know. Are you sure you're OK?'

I mustered a smile and squeezed her hand. 'You're one of the good ones, Stace. Yes, I'm fine. Just slightly ragged round the edges. Don't you worry.'

When she had gone I pulled my phone out of my pocket. *Hello Daphne, do you think we could bring our supervision session forward from Friday, please? It's fairly urgent, but not desperate.* I sent the message before I could change my mind.

Chapter 15

Some things don't ever seem to change, so it's disconcerting when they do. All my supervision had been at Daphne's house, both my early days back a decade ago and my more current sessions during this last couple of years. Originally, what she now called 'the snug' had been a dedicated practice room for her paying clients and supervisees. I remember it as being slightly austere, in my view, with unadorned walls and daunting grey metal filing cabinets. Nowadays, following Daphne's retirement, it had become a dual-purpose room, with the concession to therapy being the two chairs set centrally. The rest of the room contained handsome, book-laden shelves and a small couch, the filing cabinets having been relegated elsewhere.

But now, Daphne told me, the snug was having 'a freshen up', whatever that meant. It would have been finished by Friday, when we were supposed to be having our supervision, but since it had been brought forward to Tuesday, we would be having the session in the living room for once. All I'd ever had was a glimpse of the three-piece suite and fireplace in the living room as we passed on the way to the snug. But once inside, you could appreciate the generous proportions of the room, the deep pile carpet and the tastefully placed furnishings. This room surpassed the snug in terms of luxury and stylishness. Yet I felt stifled by the opulence rather than comfortable.

I suppose the way this change of room threw me off balance was a measure of my jitteriness. I was all too aware that this was not going to be a normal supervision, which had always been stimulating and reaffirming, but more akin to a Catholic-style confession. I wondered with some foreboding what my penance would be.

I jumped in before Daphne could say anything and thanked her for changing the time of our session at such short notice. She responded briefly, then straightaway said, 'Now then, Simon.

What's this all about?'

So there was to be no small talk, no asking me how I was, no chat to ease me in. I took a deep breath. 'It's about a situation that has arisen between myself and a client. You might remember last time I came here I told you that I was about to start seeing a repeat client who had contacted me again wanting some more sessions.' I carried on to remind Daphne about the history of Fleur's case. She interrupted with a nod and told me she had refreshed her memory from the notes of our last session. There was a briskness about Daphne today.

'Since you and I last met I've seen this client twice,' I said. I gave Daphne a concise summary of the first session. I spoke of how I could see that the client had been making satisfactory and normal progress towards life restoration, such as forming a new alliance with a friend and moving house. She was having some difficulty with the adjustment to living in a new home. I reported the encounter with a man who strongly reminded her of her deceased husband and how that had unnerved her, thus precipitating her request for more therapy. I could see that Daphne was listening carefully, but she didn't interrupt.

I moved on to the second session. I said how Fleur had taken on board our discussion about accepting and settling in to her new location, and how she went on to bring up and talk openly about her experiences with internet dating. I reported that she was invested in finding a man online who resembled her deceased husband. Then I related how she had also disclosed that she continued to search in her area for the husband look-alike and had eventually seen him again in the park. I said she had made the cryptic remark to me, "I don't know what he'd think about my hair being cut off", which there wasn't time to discuss in the session, beyond me asking her if this was a game she was playing. Daphne sought several clarifications of what I'd just told her, such as the significance of the cut hair. She referred to Fleur looking for the Michael look-alike as 'stalking'. I didn't think that was quite the right term, because the man was totally unaware of

136

Fleur, but I didn't want to argue.

'In conclusion, currently you don't know what the client's mind state was when she made the remark about her hair. When is your next appointment with her?' I told her that it was Friday morning. 'Have you asked to have our supervision session now so that we can discuss this before you see her? Also you mentioned a "situation".'

This was it. I let my eyes slide away from her face and focussed on the embossed wallpaper just above her shoulder. 'Last Saturday I happened to be walking through the town where the client lives and I saw her come out of a shop. She was only a short distance in front of me and she spotted me at the same time. We both said hello and exchanged a few pleasantries. I was as surprised to see her as she was to see me. We chatted for a couple of minutes and then we decided to go and have a cup of tea in a café.' There was a glass of water on the table next to me and I gulped at it.

'What do you mean, "you decided"? Who mentioned it first?'

I admitted that the suggestion was mine. 'Go on,' she said.

I sighed. Hedging and telling evasive half-truths clearly wasn't going to get me through, although I hadn't been truthful about why I had bumped into Fleur. I told her that we talked affably in the café for about half an hour and I offered her a lift home. One there she invited me to see inside her house. Since she had talked about it a lot, I accepted.

Before I could say more there was a shuffling and a plaintive meowing at the door. Montagu. For once I was glad of the interruption, because immediately Daphne transferred her attention to him. Then I noticed that one of his front paws was bandaged and he was limping as he held the damaged paw off the ground.

'Poor Montagu,' said Daphne, helping him up off the floor onto her lap. I enquired what had happened and she told me that the vet said his paw had been badly bitten, almost certainly by another cat. 'You're getting too old to fight with the big boys, aren't you, darling?'

I commiserated. Indeed he did look sorry for himself. His normal haughty expression seemed to have been replaced by a pitiful, chastened demeanour. Anyway, I had other things to think about than a middle-aged cat.

After Montagu had been dispatched, Daphne asked me what happened after I went into Fleur's house. I gave an account of how she had shown me round downstairs and in the garden, how we'd looked at photographs and at Michael's hat, and how she had made tea and we talked some more in a friendly manner.

'At any time did it occur to you that it was inappropriate to go with her to a café and inside her house?'

'Yes.'

'And yet you continued?'

'Yes.'

Daphne, her hands clasped loosely in her lap as usual, waited for me to say more. When I didn't, she said, 'Why did you do this, Simon?'

I spread my hands. 'I was enjoying her company. She was enjoying mine too, I believe. When I came to take my leave…' I stopped. There was going to be no way I could sugar-coat this. 'When I came to take my leave I hugged her for a couple of minutes and I kissed her cheek.' The memory was still clear of her body in my arms and her breath on my neck. 'That was all that happened. I said I would see her at the next appointment this Friday and I left.'

I could feel my face getting hot. I forced myself to look at Daphne. She hadn't moved. She sat perfectly still, impeccably dressed as ever, her face inscrutable. 'Is there anything else you need to tell me?'

It was as if she could look into my mind. 'Nothing else about that particular day, but there is something else.' I licked my lips and slurped at the water, nearly spilling it down my front. 'When the client told me she had signed up to a particular internet dating site, she also told me her username. I didn't ask her - she just volunteered the information. Well, I looked at her profile on the website. I learned a lot more about her than what had come up in our sessions.' I couldn't keep looking at Daphne while I said the next bit so I looked down at the carpet between us. 'It did occur to me that I could set up a bogus profile on the site and... and send her a message. But it was only a fleeting idea. I didn't act on it. And that's everything.' I felt numb, empty. At least it was all out now.

'Simon, do you realise how utterly stupid you have been?'

She wasn't beating about the bush. 'I know it was outside the rules, but... it just seemed to happen.' I knew I was being disingenuous, and she knew it too.

'Do you have sexual feelings towards this woman?'

I squirmed. 'It's not that simple. I feel... *protective* towards her. She seems so delicate. And let me say she has absolutely not made any advances towards me. She is just pleasant and open.'

'And so you took advantage of the situation. A situation you should never have been in in the first place, with a vulnerable person who is at best subject to unrealistic fantasies and at worst has mental health issues.'

God. This was worse than I thought it would be. To my horror, I felt sobs welling up in my throat.

'Has is occurred to you that she might report the incident?'

That did it. Daphne silently passed me a box of tissues and I snuffled into one, glad to have my face covered. I hadn't cried since Grandad died. 'Sorry,' I said. Daphne waited while I composed myself. 'I don't think she would report what happened. She didn't seem offended at all. It was she who suggested I came into her house, and she didn't pull away when I held her.'

'She could relate the events to a friend who might see it from a different perspective and encourage her to take the matter further. Apart from the breach of trust with the client, do you see how this could escalate and affect both your career and the

139

reputation of The Willows?'

Yes, of course I could see. And I should have known better. I *had* known better; I had thought I could get away with it, and my infatuation had blocked everything else out. I moved in my chair and eased my tense shoulders.

Daphne shuffled too, stretching out her gnarled fingers and rubbing each hand. 'I think we should take a break. Would you like a hot drink?' Her voice was less harsh now.

This was a departure, and a welcome one, from the established business-like custom of our supervision sessions. But then, this was scarcely a normal session. I used the time Daphne was out of the room to stand up and do a few shoulder rolls and try to get myself back to some semblance of calm after my emotional response. I listened to the sounds coming from the kitchen: a kettle coming to the boil, a cupboard door closing, a lid unscrewing, the chink of a teaspoon on the side of a cup, Daphne's special voice that she used to address Montagu. Then there was the fridge opening and closing, recognisably different to the cupboard noise. Comforting everyday sounds.

Daphne hobbled in with the tray and I rushed with concern to help her. After we were settled she said, 'Thank you for being frank with me, Simon. Now what we have to do is work out a way forward. I am supposed to report this, you know.'

I took in her pensive expression. 'I did come here of my own free will as soon as I could after the... the incident.' It was the best I could offer in my defence.

She sat nursing her coffee cup. Was she considering her options? She held my career in her hands in that moment.

'I am so, so sorry for my behaviour. Nothing like this will ever happen again.' It sounded glib; I could hear it myself as I said it.

'The foremost thing is damage limitation to the client. Of course you absolutely must not see her again, and she will have to be informed that her session with you – Friday, isn't it? – will be cancelled and that you cannot engage with her again because

140

of the rules that were infringed. Is that clear?'

I bowed my head so that she would not see my expression. Yes, it was clear and inevitable. The wretchedness of it all would hit me later, no doubt.

'If I can be sure that you will sever your connection with the client, it's my decision that the greater good would be served by me not reporting this issue. You are an excellent therapist, Simon, one of the best it's been my privilege to work with, and it would be a loss to the profession for your career to be marred by one incident.'

I gasped out my thanks. Oh, the relief!

She looked at me with more kindness than she had all afternoon. 'Now, let's discuss you. You've made some serious errors of judgement, which is unusual for you. I can see how much of a toll this has taken on you and I strongly recommend that you take some time off. Then, after you come back, we can explore further just why you allowed this to happen. Let's see, I don't think you've had a holiday this year, have you?'

I told her that as luck would have it I had two weeks' leave starting this weekend. She asked what my plans were and I told her that I didn't have any fixed plans, but I would definitely go away somewhere. She said she remembered, now that I'd reminded her, that I was going on holiday with my girlfriend.

I licked my lips. 'That's not happening now. I think the relationship is finished. You see…' I decided to get it off my chest. 'When I was at the client's house, I should have been at Cora's art exhibition, her first one. It was very important to her, and it's unforgivable that I should have missed it. I just lost track of the time.'

Daphne sighed. 'Oh, Simon. Use your time off well. You need to.'

It was as she was showing me out that I said, 'It wasn't quite true when I said I had lost track of the time at the client's house. I could have looked at my phone to check it. But I didn't.'

*

I saw the supermarket carrier bag on my doorstep as soon as I got out of the lift. I suppose I should have guessed what was in it. When I got inside my flat I delved into the bag and found the spare pyjamas and slippers that I used to keep at Cora's, a toothbrush, shaving stuff and other toiletries, various CDs and a couple of books. No note.

Chapter 16

I can't say I was comfortable, sitting in my car, a little way up the road from Fleur's house. I knew I shouldn't have been there. This pleasant suburb, with its trees and tidy houses, didn't take kindly to loiterers like me. Even though it was a residential area, there were a fair number of cars travelling up and down the street – probably because it was five-thirty, and people were coming home from work. I watched as Fleur's neighbours, presumably the young couple that she had mentioned, reversed up in front of their house and opened the hatchback of their car to unload shopping, perhaps the weekly groceries from one of the local big stores. They heaved several large bags out of the boot, chatting together as they did so. I wondered what they were talking about: an anecdote from work? what they were going to have for their tea? what they would watch on TV tonight? They seemed like nice people, anyway.

A child was riding a bike with stabilisers along the pavement, while his mother guided his wobbly progress from behind. I didn't think Fleur would be home from work yet, which is why I was lurking there, so I was surprised to see a car on the hardstanding in front of her window. I thought I remembered her saying that she drove to work, but I wasn't sure. Another car was parked on the road outside, effectively blocking her in. I felt like a private detective, viewing the neighbourhood comings and goings like this. I'd be on my way soon.

I'd had two days to reflect on my time with Daphne. So how did I feel? Chastened, embarrassed, shamefaced, sorry, guilty, relieved, cleansed, sore, freed, sad, confused, disoriented? All of the above? I'd started jotting the words down as they came to me, as part of my move to get ahead of the game before I had to dissect the whole sorry business with Daphne in our next session. I knew that my list contained a lot of contradictions, but that was about the size of it.

In my career I hadn't as yet felt called to qualify and practice as a supervisor. Why was that, I wonder? I'd got more than enough experience under my belt. Maybe it had been because in general I felt fulfilled and challenged enough with my day-to-day work. But now, funnily enough, the last session with Daphne and her adroit handling of it, had brought home to me anew how important supervision was, and that it was about time I aspired to doing some. *Adroit...* that was an understatement. I had gone over the session in my mind several times, including the painful bits. Well, it was all painful, but getting less so with each airing in my mind. I really took my hat off to Daphne. Yes, she had given me a real bollocking, but it was no less than I deserved. After that she had been kind and constructive. She had stuck her neck out for me by not making a formal report of the issue, and I was fulfilling my part by not engaging with Fleur again. I was pretty confident – no, I was sure – that Fleur would not make a complaint. For the hundredth time I counted my blessings that I had Daphne as a supervisor. Next time I saw her I would take her a bunch of flowers.

As yet my own feelings were too mixed up, sore and new to address them properly. Having all the tools and experience of counselling and psychotherapy should mean you can apply it to yourself, but it rarely works out that way. Though I could say the main feeling that was emerging from the mess inside my head was relief. It had all been nipped in the bud before it could do any damage to Fleur or to my career. What was far less clear was the entanglement in my mind between the end of the two relationships – with Cora and with Fleur.

So what was I doing sitting in my car close to Fleur's house, when I knew I shouldn't be here? Well, it had seemed so cold, so impersonal for her to be notified by email that our sessions were henceforth terminated. I had wanted to put through her door a short note, a handwritten note, wishing her well. I admitted to myself that this desire was as much for me as for her. A kind of closure, I suppose. I absolutely did not want to see her; I

144

understood well enough that was prohibited. Which was why I had arrived expecting her to be still at work. Now seeing her car on the drive put me in a state of indecision. The last thing I wanted was for her to see me and come to the door. On the other hand I could put on the light jacket that I kept in the car, put the hood up, keep my head down and be really quick.

I got out the card that I had just bought. It was simple and small, with flowers on the front and blank inside. I fished a pen out of my pocket, and after some thought I wrote: *'Fleur, this is just a short note to wish you all the best for the future. Kind regards, Simon.'* I stared at the words. Yes, it hit the right note. It was short and to the point, and it acknowledged the finality of this goodbye. I put it in the envelope and wrote her name on the outside. I held the envelope, reluctant to take the final step and put it through the door.

It was as well that I had hesitated. Her front door opened and she came out. I sank down in my seat, but I didn't think she could see me. She was talking to somebody just inside the house, somebody whom I couldn't see yet. And then the person stepped out. He was wearing the hat, Michael's hat. It was only for a couple of seconds, but disbelief and shock, utter shock, ran through me. Then I saw the dog, the black spaniel, that the man had on a lead. The dog leapt about and wagged his tail. Fleur bent down and stroked him, at the same time smiling up at the man and making some animated remark. The man opened the car door that was parked across her house front. The dog jumped into the back, Fleur got into the passenger seat and they drove off.

Chapter 17

I was heading home earlier than usual on Friday afternoon because my monthly slot with Daphne had already happened on the previous Tuesday. Due to my earlier knocking-off time the train was relatively quiet, and I watched a middle-class scene of busy roads and neat housing estates trundle past the window. Normally I would whip my phone out and start browsing straight away, but today was more of a staring apathetically out of the window kind of day.

My two-week holiday had now officially kicked off. I had said my goodbyes at work and responded cheerily to enquiries about how I was going to spend my fortnight and where I was going. Lucy was round-eyed with envy about my destination and she said she wished she could jump into my suitcase. A bit over the top, I thought. Anyway, I planned to take only a large backpack but I didn't tell her that. There had been a general tactful avoidance of asking who I was going with. I should have known better than to share with Kai that Cora and I had broken up, because it obviously hadn't taken long to do the rounds in the staff room. I was just glad that I hadn't given him any details beyond that we were calling it a day.

It was only a short walk back from the train to my flat. The box of miscellaneous stuff that Cora had dumped on my doorstep still stood on the table, along with a coffee mug, two beer cans and the remains of last night's meal. I threw the patio doors open to let in some fresh air. The flat was a mess, no two ways about it. It was never particularly spotless at the best of times, but now it had fallen below even my permissive standards. I knew I should tidy it up; I also knew I couldn't be arsed. Tomorrow, I told myself. I'd have a double blitz on cleaning up and packing for my trip. Tomorrow.

So, what to do now. I couldn't think of any friends who would be free at short notice on a Friday evening, and the fridge didn't yield up much to my inspection apart from some dubious salad and ancient cheese. I mooched about for a while, fiddling with this and that, and wondering what Cora was doing now. My fingers itched to message her. But I knew that the thought was mainly born of habit and the gap that her absence now left in my life. I grabbed my car keys and headed down to the underground carpark.

It would probably have done me more good to go for a ride on my bike, but again I couldn't make the effort. Instead I thought I would get my fresh air by taking the car out. But even my beautiful car didn't give me the buzz that it usually did. It was just a car with the top sliced off. I drove aimlessly for a while, jabbing my fingers at the radio to find some music that fitted my mood. Eventually I found some retro hard rock and I cranked the volume up. This attracted some disapproving looks from old ladies and other passers-by at traffic lights. Another day I would have either considerately moderated the sound or revelled in being a badass. Today I couldn't be bothered to do either. If Nathan had been with me he would definitely have been in the badass camp. Nathan… I could message him and see if he was doing anything this evening. Now that was a good idea. My son had been more reliably communicative, with a pleasing dose of hero worship thrown in, since I had acquired the car. Then I remembered he had told me that he was staying at a friend's place tonight. Was it tonight or tomorrow? Everything about this week was weird and distorted, including time.

On the other hand, I was in the vicinity of Lisa's house, so perhaps I could stop by and say hi to Joe. He and Lisa were likely to be there because it was getting on towards his bedtime. I was uncertain because I wasn't in the habit of dropping in unannounced, but if I phoned, Lisa might have a reason to put me off. And I was getting a bit desperate.

The end of Lisa's cul-de-sac was crammed with cars as usual, so I had to park in the next street. This was a disadvantage of having a car: having to park it somewhere. The gate to the front garden was open on this occasion, so I didn't have to push it and hear its usual irritating screech, always reminding me that I could have fixed it and hadn't ever got round to it. Front door or back door? Usually she was expecting me so back door seemed appropriate then, but today front door seemed a better choice. I rang the bell and then, uncertain if it had worked or not, I rapped on the door and listened for the approach of her footsteps.

'Simon! I thought it was Mum come early. Nothing wrong is there? Nathan's not here.' Her expression went from surprise to consternation as she said this.

'No, nothing's wrong. I was just passing and I thought I'd say hello.' I wondered if my words sounded as false to her as they did to me. I didn't acknowledge her comment about Nathan.

'Do you want to come in?' she said, after a small pause. This situation was unfamiliar for both of us. I passed through into the living room where Joe was lying on his stomach, in the time-honoured way of small children, playing with toy cars. With a jolt I recognised them as my own Dinky cars from my childhood. I had forgotten giving them to Nathan and now it seemed they had been passed onto Joe. This continuity and linkage to the past was unexpectedly pleasing. I dropped down beside Joe and picked up a yellow saloon, dull with age. I turned its wheels with my fingers and marvelled anew at the workmanship. Joe seemed to take my appearance out of nowhere totally in his stride. 'This one's got doors that open,' he informed me, passing me the little model. I wasn't sure if this particular car had been one of mine, but I duly admired it and asked him if he knew that I used to play with these cars when I was a little boy. If he was interested in that fact, he didn't show it. I felt ridiculously pleased that my cars had been passed on down the generations. But of course, Joe wasn't my son, or technically even my stepson.

'Tell Simon where you're going in a minute,' Lisa said. She had to prompt him again before he said, 'Granny's house.' I replied I thought that was nice.

'Seeing Joe with the cars has brought back memories of how

I used to lie on the floor just like this and play with these same cars,' I said, mainly to Lisa. 'I can remember playing under the table at my grandparents' house.' The clarity of the memory was striking and catapulted me back to simpler times. I could almost smell the roasting meat coming from my grandmother's kitchen and taste the rice pudding that invariably followed afterwards.

'That'll be Mum,' said Lisa, getting up to answer the ring of the doorbell. Thank God Lisa's Mum was a front-door-ring-the-bell person or she would have come straight in through the back door to find me here, which I don't think would have made her day. Or mine. I heard their muffled conversation and prayed that she wouldn't be asked in. Lisa called to Joe, which he ignored. I urged him to leave his cars and go to see Granny. I assured him that I would look after them for him. He got up abruptly and ran out, very Joe-like. I sat on the sofa and listened to the conversation, which was largely about what Joe had in his bag to take to Granny's. I daresay Lisa had mouthed to her mother that I was there.

I sat back and gazed around me. It had been a long time since I had been on my own here and therefore able to take it in properly. I saw a cluttered room of shabby comfort and toy-filled family life. The three-piece suite had seen better days, as had the carpet. In fact, it was almost threadbare in some places. I realised that Lisa must find it hard to make ends meet. And there was I with an expensive sports car parked outside, bought on a whim.

I heard the front door open again, and Lisa instructing Joe to be good for Granny and to say goodbye to Simon. He came scurrying back into the room, threw himself onto my lower half and gave me a quick but definite hug, before running out again without saying anything. Two hugs in as many weeks! You never knew with Joe.

*

When Lisa came back I stood up, ready to take my leave. I didn't feel as if I could string it out now that Joe had gone.

Besides which, she probably had things to do. But she offered me a drink, so after a token hesitation I asked for a coffee.

'Are you sure? I'm having some wine and you're welcome to join me.' This time my hesitation was more real because I was driving, but I decided that one glass would be OK. Another definite disadvantage of having a car is needing to watch your alcohol intake.

Lisa brought in two glasses and a bottle. She settled herself in an armchair opposite me, curled her legs up under her, and we drank in awkward silence. What on earth was I doing here? But then, she had asked me to stay after Joe had left. Maybe she was just being polite.

I started to make some remark about Joe and his cars at the same time as she started talking. We both stopped, embarrassed. I insisted that she should go ahead. 'That was a brilliant day we had in Brighton. Joe talked a lot about it afterwards. I'm really grateful that you took us.'

'It wasn't exactly planned, but yes, it did work out well. Perhaps we should do something like that again one day.'

'Maybe.' We both looked away and sipped our wine, leaving that idea hanging.

'Is there anything wrong?' said Lisa. 'You seem, I don't know, a bit down.'

I put my glass on the coffee table so I wouldn't drink it too quickly. 'I've made a total mess of everything.' That about covered it.

'What's happened?' Lisa's face, bless her, was filled with consternation and concern.

How could I put it, given that most of it was confidential? 'I've made an error at work. I behaved unprofessionally with a client, a female client. I went and made a clean breast of it all to my supervisor. She, luckily for me, has decided not to take it further. But it's really thrown me off balance.'

'When you say you "behaved unprofessionally", what exactly do you mean?' She was looking more wary now.

'Oh, not what you're thinking. Basically I bumped into her when I was out and we went to a café and then to her house.' It seemed best to tell her the edited version and omit the parts about the dating website and me purposely cruising around where Fleur lived. But I did add that I had developed feelings for her.

'What feelings? You mean you fancied her?'

'Well, sort of, but it's more subtle than that. It's hard to put into words, but the closest I can get is that I wanted to protect her and keep her safe. She seemed so... so delicate and yet brave, and that seemed to press a button in me. You hear of therapists getting involved with their clients, but it's never happened to me like this before.'

'Have you told your girlfriend what you're telling me?'

I groaned. 'That's the other thing. The time when I was supposed to be at Cora's first art exhibition, which was a really big deal for her and had been planned for weeks, I was at Fl... I was at my client's house. So, Cora's finished with me. No brainer, isn't it? Even though perhaps she and I were running out of steam in our relationship, it was really shitty of me to do what I did. So you see, I've really fucked up.' I picked up my glass and found it was empty. I must have been drinking and hardly noticed. Lisa picked up the bottle to give us both a refill. I put my hand over my glass. 'I can't. I'm driving.'

'Oh, that's a shame.' She paused. 'Look, you could sleep in Nathan's bed tonight. I think we could both do with a drink.'

I didn't need much persuading, and I glugged at my refilled glass.

'Oh, Simon. I'm sorry that you're having such a rough time.'

She did indeed seem full of sympathy as she sat there with her bare feet, old jeans and baggy T-shirt. I was touched by how supportive she was being and I told her so. I had more or less barged into her home and she had made me welcome; I was quite overwhelmed. She quizzed me more on the whole sorry story and I filled her in on such gaps as I could. Especially she asked

151

about my relationship with Cora and was it really over. She said she'd always been curious about her, but not felt it was her place to ask questions. Did I detect some jealousy there?

'You never said much about her,' Lisa had said, 'but I got the impression that she was quite snooty and arty-farty, at least that was what Nathan implied, and it didn't sound like you two had much in common.'

My immediate reaction was to jump to Cora's defence, but I well remembered that awful toe-curling time when we went out for lunch with Nathan. She had been pretty defensive then, and not showing her best side. 'Oh, we had enough in common to keep us going. You know, meals, clubs, theatre, that sort of thing. And she was witty and sparkling. But the relationship had got sort of... stuck. We had two or three dates a week, and neither of us wanted more than that, or to change our living arrangements.' I could have added that Cora was arresting to look at and enthusiastic in bed, but I tactfully kept that to myself.

'Were – or are - you in love with her?'

Well, that was the million dollar question, wasn't it, and I groped for an honest answer. 'No, not really. We liked each other and had a good time, but I wouldn't say I was in love with her. So I suppose it's inevitable that it would run its course.'

I was quite surprised that she was more interested in what had happened with Cora than with Fleur. Maybe that was because she had dismissed the Fleur situation as a passing infatuation and aberration, which I suppose it was, whereas Cora had been a girlfriend and part of my life, as Lisa herself had been once. Interesting. Could I myself view the situation like that? I was dimly aware that another level of interpretation had flickered into my mind. I'd think about it another time.

Lisa picked up the wine bottle, which seemed to have emptied itself. 'Neither of us is going anywhere,' she said. 'Shall we open another? There's not much to eat, but I can manage some cheese and pickle sandwiches.'

I sat back and closed my eyes while she was in the kitchen,

feeling a blessed relaxation seeping over me that wasn't just the wine. For the first time since my session with Daphne I felt the cloud of gloom and confusion that had enveloped me start to melt away a little. Lisa reappeared with sandwiches, crisps and another bottle tucked under her arm. She apologised that it was only white bread, but that's all the boys would eat. I realised that I was ravenous and I said, with my mouth full, that she always had been an ace sandwich maker.

We fell into talking about the boys, which was our default mode. They had both settled back into the school term OK. Nathan was spending more time with the friend whose house he was at now, who seemed to be a well-behaved lad. I sat back, restored to something nearer to normality after the confessions, alcohol and food. I felt quite drunk, having sunk a few glasses on an empty stomach. The world definitely seemed more benign now.

Lisa's calm acceptance and sympathetic listening had meant a lot, and I told her so. I looked at her more attentively now. Did she seemed a bit subdued, or was she just relaxed? 'With me going on so much about my troubles, I'm sorry I haven't asked anything about you. So how are you doing?'

'I'm OK.' Her smile wasn't quite convincing.

'Are you sure?'

She waved her glass dismissively. 'Oh, it's just that I was dumped this afternoon. We were supposed to be going out for a meal tonight but then he sent a text calling it all off. You can see if you like.' She passed me her phone.

Of course. If I hadn't been wrapped up in myself so much the penny would have dropped: Joe fixed up to go to her mother's and Nathan away, yet she wasn't going out. I looked at the text: *"Lisa, I think we should bring our relationship to a close. I would like to broaden my horizons and see other people. Nevertheless, these last few weeks have been fun and I wish you all the best for your future. P."*

What a twat. I was about to say that to Lisa when I realised that my behaviour with Cora cast me in the same category.

153

Instead I said, 'Well, he certainly doesn't mince his words. And to do it just a few hours before you were supposed to be going out is pretty cold.' Again, I knew I was being a hypocrite. 'Did you see it coming at all?'

She shook her head. 'I thought it was all going quite well. I met his two kids last week. Maybe that had something to do with it? Perhaps they didn't like me.' She went on to tell me that he was recently divorced, an architect, and she had met him online. Good old internet dating. He lived in an upmarket four bedroomed, detached house about ten miles away. He hadn't yet met Nathan and Joe. I wondered if he had a sports car like mine. I wouldn't be surprised. I couldn't help speculating if he was good in bed, but it wasn't my business to enquire.

'I'm so sorry. You don't deserve that.'

'Thanks for that, but it's OK. It was just a shock, that's all. It's not that I expected it to last for very long.' She fished a handkerchief out of her pocket and sniffled into it. 'I knew really I wasn't good enough for him. Not being good enough seems to have been the story of my life.'

'Oh, come here!' It was sheer impulse and compassion that made me say that and I held out my arms to her. She hesitated a moment, then scuttled over to the sofa and fitted herself against me, burying her head in my shoulder. I held her close and absorbed her tears in my shirt. The last time I had held her like this must have been before we split up. Yet the memory of how she had felt when she was snuggled against me was reactivated in an instant.

'You were never "not good enough" for me.' I was appalled that she thought that. 'What happened was my fault. You know I never liked living with your mother, and I couldn't see an end to it. So I bottled it and took the easy way out.'

'I know I wasn't always very easy to live with either, being cooped up with a toddler all day.' Her voice was muffled against my side. Memories that I don't often dwell on nowadays flashed into my mind: the claustrophobia of our room with Nathan's cot

154

squeezed into the corner, talking in whispers and trying to subdue Nathan's crying so as not to disturb anyone else. The way that the bubbly, fun-loving girl that I had married gradually turned into a whining drudge. The arguments that we hissed at each other. The petty house rules that I railed against. The feeling of frustration and inadequacy that I wasn't ready for all this responsibility.

I pushed the memories back into the past, where they belonged. 'Let's just say it was a bad time all round for us.'

'Would it have been different if we'd had our own place, do you think?'

'I'm sure it would. If Nathan had come along a few years later, when we were established, it would all have been different.'

She had stayed quietly cuddled up against me and I could feel her breathing. 'I'm so sorry that I let you down. But never, ever, think that it was because you weren't good enough.' I stroked her hair, feeling its soft waves under my fingers. 'You have lovely hair,' I told her.

'It's just ordinary hair.'

'That's why I like it.' I buried my nose in it and smelled her scalp. 'I've never loved another woman since you, you know.'

'I haven't loved anyone else either.'

We sat quietly. I was dimly aware that this was irregular, yet did it matter? It was a balm that we both needed at that time.

Eventually she sat up. 'By the way,' I said. 'What does the P stand for? You've never said his name.'

She was drinking her last glass of wine and her reply was indistinct. I had to ask her to repeat it.

'Piers?' I said doubtfully.

She nodded, avoiding my eyes.

'*Piers?* I felt the guffaw starting in my throat and I didn't even try to control it. 'What a poncy name!' I put my head back and laughed until my belly ached. No wonder she'd never mentioned it. She picked up a cushion and hit me with it. I wrestled it off her and we both fell in a heap laughing.

Chapter 18

The first thing I was aware of was the lack of noise. At my place there was always the hum of traffic even on a Saturday morning. I opened my eyes and had that strange, disoriented feeling you get when for just a couple of seconds you don't know where you are. The sun was trying to make its way in through the thin curtains which Lisa had drawn across the window last night. I blinked. Understandably, I hadn't taken much notice of the room then. Now I looked round and saw a dressing table cluttered with perfumes, creams and other girly stuff, and a small TV mounted on the wall. A dress was hanging up on the door of the adjacent wardrobe. Perhaps it was what she had been going to wear last night for her date.

I reached my arm over to the empty side of the bed and found it still warm from her body. I left my hand there. If it weren't for the lingering warmth that I was savouring, I could have imagined that what happened last night was just a dream. When I had turned up at Lisa's house last night, never in a million years would I have imagined that the evening would end as it had. All I had been looking for was a distraction from my gloom. And it was so strange; the Lisa that I had made love to had been both an exciting stranger and my familiar wife from more than a decade ago, all at once. I felt the lift off in my groin as I wished this enigmatic woman were still here beside me.

On the other hand, it was probably better that she had got up because I couldn't say that I was feeling my best. My head was woolly and achy, and my mouth felt like the bottom of a hamster cage. In other words, I'd got a classic stage one hangover. I heard a door close and footsteps going down the stairs, so I made my way to the bathroom and swallowed a plastic mug full of water. That should kick start the rehydration process. I splashed my face with water then looked at myself in the mirror and grimaced. I eyed up the three toothbrushes. One was small and had a cartoon dinosaur on it, obviously Joe's. Of the other two, the one that was driest was presumably Nathan's. He'd never know, would he, if I borrowed it? My conscience teased me, then I decided against it and settled for a dab of toothpaste on my finger rubbed around my mouth.

Lisa, sat at the kitchen table, was bundled in a pink dressing-gown, her hair delightfully tangled. She was nursing a steaming mug of coffee and staring at the screen of her phone. We wished each other a somewhat formal good morning and she asked if I wanted coffee. Good and strong, I told her. We sat at the table and eyed each other nervously. The elephant in the room shifted his grey bulk. This was surreal, sitting here and suddenly feeling as shy as I did. I tried to tell myself that this was Lisa, the familiar mother of my son, and that everything was fundamentally the same. Except that it wasn't.

'Last night was incredible,' I said, aware that it sounded like a cliché. I reached across the table to take her hand.

She pulled away from me. 'It should never have happened. I don't know what we were thinking.'

'There wasn't much thinking went into it, was there? But surely you felt it was pretty amazing, like I did. More than just casual sex. Go on, admit it.' That Piers must have been off his head, I thought.

'Yes, it was amazing... that's part of what's so confusing. But Simon, it was just a one-off. We must forget all about it and go back to normal now.'

I reached over the table again and took her hand more firmly this time, feeling more confident now that she had admitted to the magic that had exploded between us. 'Must we go back to how we were? Or did we discover an extraordinary opportunity yesterday?'

'What do you mean?'

To me the way seemed suddenly clear, but I could see she was in turmoil, so I said, 'Look, I know we're both on the rebound, so you have to allow for that. But yesterday was the first time in ages, years probably, that we've been together for some time without either of the boys and look what happened. And you were so kind and understanding to me.'

'You were kind to me too. But you can't blame me for being cautious.' She turned her face away from me. 'You hurt me deeply once. You *abandoned* me and Nathan. I can't risk being hurt like that again.'

She spoke with quiet dignity and it stabbed afresh that I had inflicted so much damage on her. A voice inside me said that it wasn't all my fault, but now was not the time to apportion blame. We'd done enough of that years ago. I stroked her hand. 'Perhaps I've never realised the true depth of the injury to you and I apologise from the bottom of my heart. But now, we seem to have found a new connection. Perhaps we could start cautiously and see how it goes. And the boys would love it if we got back together. It's not unheard of, you know. I once worked with a client who –'

'I'm not one of your clients. Don't go all counsellor on me.'

'Sorry.' She'd never liked that and I should have known better, but sometimes it's my default thinking mode.

'I'll make some toast,' she said, getting up and fumbling with the bread. I got up too and put my arms around her. Oh, the smell of her, the feel of her. For a moment she tensed and I thought she was going to push me away, but then she relaxed and leant into me. Take it gently, I instructed myself. Give her confidence, don't scare her. Don't you dare mess this up.

'I'm going to woo you,' I whispered in her ear. 'You see if I don't. I'll take you out to dinner, I'll buy you gifts, I'll… I'll love you.' There, I'd said it. 'We can meet clandestinely at first if you like, like secret lovers. It will be fun, I promise.'

'This is all too much to take in,' she said. 'My head is spinning.'

I released her. 'Yes, it's like a miracle. Tell you what, I'm going away tomorrow for two weeks, as you know. That gives us both a chance to stand back and think it over. You know how I feel: that it's worth us giving it a try. Not as the old Lisa and Simon, but as the new people we have become.'

She nodded, but I could see she wasn't totally convinced. 'OK. But we tell the boys nothing, right? No hinting, absolutely nothing.'

'Of course. Their welfare comes first, like it always has.' I risked giving her a kiss on the cheek. 'I'm back two weeks tomorrow. Come and meet me at the airport. Go on.'

She wouldn't promise, but she didn't refuse outright either. 'I'll message you anyway,' I said.

'No.' She was firm about that. 'Don't bombard me. Let's give each other space.'

I agreed, at first reluctantly, but then seeing that it might not be such a bad idea.

The doorbell made us both jump. 'Oh shit, that'll be Mum bringing Joe home. I don't want her finding you here and me in my dressing gown. Can you slip out quietly through the back door?'

We whispered our goodbyes like the conspirators we were. I waited until I heard the front door closing before I nipped smartly down the path, leaving the noisy gate open. I was grinning all over my face as I unlocked my car. Who would have thought it? A whole new life vista was tentatively opening up for me. Of course, everything has its downsides: if Lisa and I got back together, I would have to be nice to her mother.

Chapter 19

It was only once I was on the plane and we were airborne that the trip became real to me. The trolley had travelled down the aisle at its normal snail's pace – why does it always seem so slow? – and now I sat with a gin and tonic, correctly served with ice and lemon, in front of me. Such a drink would never pass my lips at home, but here, in this suspended between-world, it seemed to hit the spot.

I had exchanged pleasantries with the couple next me, a cheery middle-aged pair with all the mannerisms of the long married who I felt would whip out photos of their grandchildren given half a chance. So I had ostentatiously flourished my Kindle and fixed my eyes on the screen. A memory stirred; ah yes, Fleur had said there was a chatty woman sitting next to her on her journey to revisit El Médano.

This all felt weird. Well, the last few days had been one of the strangest periods in my life, so no surprise, really. And there was another reason. I had never in my entire life flown anywhere on my own, or indeed taken a holiday on my own. This had occurred to me yesterday while I was dragging out my old large capacity backpack from the depths of the wardrobe, which I believe had last been used when I was doing the Duke of Edinburgh Award before I left school. I spent a few minutes wondering if I should ditch the idea of travelling with this musty old relic, but once I had put some weight in it and strapped it on, the feel of it on my shoulders came flooding back. It felt much more the right thing to take than one of those suitcases that roll along on wheels. I wasn't a businessman.

The woman next to me rustled in her bag and pulled out a bar of chocolate. She offered me a piece which I declined, but she had secured her opportunity to start a conversation. Perhaps she felt it her job to take me under her wing, seeing as I was on my own, and therefore an object of curiosity at best, pity at worst.

She asked me which resort I was going to, and I have to admit to quite enjoying her perplexity when I said I wasn't going to a resort, nor staying with friends. I didn't have any accommodation booked at all, in fact. So, having established myself as a man of mystery, I politely turned back to my Kindle. It's not that I'm antisocial, but I had wanted to sink into this protected four hours in the air. I had a lot to think about, not least where I was going to head for when I stepped off the plane.

I had the window seat because my co-passengers had asked if I minded them sitting near the aisle so they could get out to the toilet. That suited me. I've always been fascinated by looking out of the window of a plane and seeing the map-like aerial view of the earth below me. We'd traversed France, cut across northern Spain and then made our way over miles of vast blue ocean. And now we were beginning our descent and the island crept into view. Yes, I was going to Tenerife. Well, it was as good a place as any at short notice wasn't it?

Crowds jostled outside the Arrivals Hall and couples – it seemed like mainly couples – with mountainous trolleys of luggage made their way to long lines of waiting coaches, having been directed there by reps in their colourful uniforms. I could have taken a safe option like that: two catered, cosseted weeks lying in the sun. Daphne had suggested that I needed to reflect, and I could have done that whilst being waited on. But things had moved on since my last time with Daphne; the whole thing about my misdemeanour with Fleur had been eclipsed by more recent events. More than simply reflection, I felt I needed a change, something different. Adventure, even. Just being here on my own with nowhere fixed to stay was a step outside my comfort zone for me, for conventional, staid Simon who had even struggled not so long ago with going to work not wearing a tie.

*

I had enjoyed the first four days of my holiday, in an

161

otherworldly sort of way. When I had first arrived, I had stood outside the airport and surrendered to the novelty of not knowing where I was headed. This was the Simon who drove a sports car, not the middle-of-the-road one who had a responsible career. A large bus that stated its destination as Santa Cruz had glided in. I vaguely knew that was the name of Tenerife's capital, so I went for it. Not much more than an hour later I was standing in an authentic Spanish city with hardly any tourists in sight, just local Spanish people. I worked out that they were local because they were wearing sweaters and jackets rather than T-shirts. I asked my way to the Tourist Information centre and booked a modest hotel. After settling in, I set off to explore the city on foot, my money belt cosy against my midriff – another thing that had come back to me from my short teenage backpacking days. I sat in a bar and allowed myself to embrace the paradox of the disorientation you always get on the first day that you travel and the dizzying freedom that I was actually here, on my own, and able to do whatever I wanted.

Santa Cruz turned out to be an interesting place. The weather was warm, I saw the city sights including an architecturally amazing Auditorio and, best of all, I took a trip to the mountains in the north of the island and spent a day hiking. I managed to suspend all serious thinking, although I'm not sure if that was a judicious decision or if my life was just too much of a bloody mess to contemplate. What I did come to realise by the end of the third day, while I sat eating my solitary dinner, was that it was time to move on. Where to, though? Of course I knew the answer. I'd always known, but I was putting it off and pretending I had come to Tenerife only because it was a popular destination and there were cheap flights going. Yet Fleur had made a good job of selling El Médano as a destination for discerning people who wanted somewhere quirky, distinctly Spanish and laid back. I wanted to see for myself.

I was shocked when I totted up how much it was going to cost to continue staying in hotels. In keeping with my newly adopted hippy persona, it occurred to me that a hostel might be an option for the rest of my holiday. But I had lost my nerve when it came to just turning up and taking my chances. Instead I Googled the options and booked a bed in a shared room – again not part of my experience since my teens - in El Médano for the rest of my trip.

I'd forgotten about the advantages of travelling with a backpack. Your hands were free, the weight was distributed evenly and you could have it with you when you were on a bus. On this particular journey, from Santa Cruz heading south, the bus was quiet enough for me to have the pack alongside me on the seat, my arm draped casually over it. The scenery was not that inspiring, to be honest. Yes, to my left there was sea, but some industrialisation too, whereas on my right the greenish slopes gave way to increasingly scrub-like vegetation on arid hillsides.

It's always strange when you see for the first time somewhere that you only know second-hand, such as by reading about it or someone else's descriptions. I stood on the plaza in El Médano and looked around me, trying to match my expectations with the reality. The iconic hotel where Fleur had stayed was unmissable, as was Montaña Roja at the opposite end of the bay. Its name was a bit of a misnomer since it was nowhere near the height of a true mountain. Nevertheless its shape cut a dramatic profile against the sky and I resolved to climb up it soon.

In my hostel I had the top bunk in a room for four people, with a shared bathroom. There was somewhere to put my stuff and that was about it. I had to remind myself that I had chosen this. My spirits lifted when I explored the kitchen and the communal areas, which were clean and bright, if somewhat minimally furnished. A couple of guys in shorts and flip-flops sat on the terrace with beers, and they said hi to me. I had turned away to go when one of them called out and asked if I'd like to join them. Why not, I thought. They were British, aged early twenties, I would say, and both medical students. They filled me in on the house rules and some tips about El Médano.

'It's a really chilled place,' said the one with a beard whose name was Dan. 'And not many families. I guess the way the wind can whip along the sand puts them off.'

I asked them if they had done any windsurfing. 'Not yet,' said the other one, who was called Liam. 'Got it booked for tomorrow. There's a few more things we want to do while we're here, like, perhaps see the stars at Mount Teide and hiring some bikes.'

'And see the Auditorio at Santa Cruz. That's up there as a must-see in Tenerife,' said Dan.

That was my cue to tell them that I had just come from Santa Cruz and to tell them my impressions. I confirmed that the Auditorio was terrific. I managed to be quite nonchalant and pretend that I was used to travelling alone. They didn't ask me about myself, which I took to be politeness rather than lack of interest. We finished our beers and I left before I risked outstaying my welcome. Still, I was cheered that they were friendly and took me as I was.

I walked along the boardwalk and tried to get a feel for the little town. My first thought was how unattractive a lot of it was. The buildings were ill assorted, cramped and jumbled, with no sense of planning or visual appeal, and there was hardly anything green. It had the hallmarks of a town, rather than a resort. For one thing there were no sprawling hotels in manicured grounds with swimming pools. There was only the Hotel Médano with its graceful white curves, built out to sea on mighty pillars. I did find a second hotel when I walked the full extent of the town along the seashore. And here were the famous windsurfers, taking advantage of the stiff breeze that was blowing. I sat down on the dark-coloured sand and let it all soak in. Had Fleur sat here like this, perhaps watching for Michael while he windsurfed? Thinking about her made me feel uncomfortable, yet I knew it was one of the reasons why I was here. I would ponder on the mistakes I had made, I would arrive at my own closure.

But not today.

*

On my first morning in El Médano I knew what I had to do straightaway: buy some earplugs. My room mates turned out to be Lars and Sven from Sweden who were here to windsurf and an older Spanish guy, by which I mean in his fifties. He was taciturn, and his English wasn't good, although it was certainly better than my non-existent Spanish. Anyway, he could have raised the roof with his snoring. The Swedes didn't seem to notice, but I spent a fitful night and got up next morning feeling ragged. Also I was aware that I was unnerved sleeping in close proximity to strangers. So I went to the chemist's with my mime ready, which involved feigning sleep and shaking my head then pointing in my ears, but the pharmacist spoke English and so I made my purchase without having to resort to acting. Pity, in a way.

Later that day in the hostel I saw Dan and Liam with others from their group, to whom they introduced me. They were David, Geraint, Poppy and Jessica. So that I could have something to recount, I told them my earplugs story and in so doing inadvertently revealed myself as a rookie hosteller. Apparently, earplugs are one of the first things you pack along with bug spray and toilet paper, all just in case. They teased me about my novice status which again I took as a good sign. You don't bother to tease people you don't like.

They were all heading out for a meal that evening at one of the little bars on the seafront, and they invited me along. Since I'd had a siesta to freshen myself up, I didn't have to think twice about my answer. We sat in the open air right next to the beach. The tide was in, and the sound of the sea breaking on the shore was a constant background accompaniment to our meal, along with the moonlight highlighting the breaking waves. A guy was sat cross-legged on the side of the boardwalk strumming his guitar. I was starting to see why this place could get under your skin.

I was sitting next to the girls on one side and Dan on the other. It turned out that the girls were a couple of years below the blokes in university, but they had tagged had along because Liam was Poppy's elder brother.

'So, Simon, isn't it? What's brought you to Tenerife, backpacking all on your own?' said Poppy. She was a slim, pretty girl, with short spiky hair dyed an outrageous shade of orange. She had the sort of looks you'd describe as cute; all snub nose, even white teeth and lots of smiling.

I smiled back at her. You couldn't help it. 'Someone told me about El Médano and I thought it sounded fascinating,' I said, truthfully. 'I only booked my flight three days before I came.'

'Wow,' said Poppy. 'That's really cool.' I don't know why it pleased me to get the admiration of these young people, but it did. Probably the old desire to fit in, like we all want to. And this crowd was really taking my mind off my responsibilities and concerns back home.

'What do you do for work?' This came from Jessica. She was a pleasant looking girl too, but more homely and quietly spoken than her friend. She had glossy brown hair down to her shoulders, and large glasses which made her look studious.

I'd rather hoped to get away without parading my life back home, but since I was asked outright I told them I was a psychotherapist. This was met with polite acknowledgement from the girls, but more than that from Dan.

'Did you say psychotherapist?' he said. 'That's a coincidence! I want to specialise in psychiatry after I'm qualified. Perhaps I can ask you a few things sometime.'

I said of course, but with reservation because I'm not a doctor like a psychiatrist is. I don't have a degree in medicine, I can't diagnose mental illness and I can't prescribe drugs. What I do is only talk therapy. Still, he seemed interested and I suppose I was flattered. Then the others called from the other end of the table to say what about hiring bikes in a couple of day's time to cycle up into the mountains in the interior of the island. I pricked my ears up at this and asked if I could join them. So that was another day's activity sorted. This trip was certainly delivering an antidote to my worries at home.

*

The next day the wind had dropped so it was obviously the day to hike up Montaña Roja. It was also something of a relief to get away on my own. The medical students were a jolly crowd but by the end of the previous evening as more bottles of wine became emptied they had become raucous and juvenile, which was a bit tedious. Jessica was the only one who remained more or less well-behaved and didn't join in with her friends when they chucked bread at each other up and down the table, which was started by Poppy. I didn't want to play the sensible teacher, but by eleven o'clock the age gap was showing and I'd had enough for one night.

I consider myself fairly fit, but Montaña Roja proved to be a good workout. This was mainly because the terrain was gravelly and loose, so each step was an extra effort. As I climbed, I encountered others on the same pilgrimage to the summit, both ascending and descending, and I said a cheery greeting to all of them. "Hi" seemed the best thing to say because I had discovered that El Médano's visitors were from all over. I had heard several languages spoken, including German, French and others that I couldn't be certain of, plus the native Spanish, of course. Surprisingly, there seemed to be far fewer Brits than I might have imagined, which was refreshing. I was sampling the cosmopolitan, bohemian vibe of El Médano for myself and I was glorying in it.

Getting to the top of Montaña Roja suffused me with that elated feeling you get from a bit of physical effort and achieving your goal. I surveyed the sea and town below me, set out like a

167

map. Beyond the town the real mountain that comprised the centre of the island, Mount Teide, dominated the scene. You could also see the airport just a couple of miles away, where the planes that were landing and taking off looked like toys. I wondered if Fleur and Michael had come up here and immersed themselves in the view just like me. I couldn't remember if she had said.

When I had slithered down to sea level, I found a table in a bar and ordered some tapas and a drink. It was Sunday, and just as Fleur had reported, the town had filled up with people, mainly families, from other parts of the island like Santa Cruz, I guessed. Many were strolling on the boardwalk and taking in the informal street entertainment like I was, the tumblers, jugglers, musicians and what have you. I was shocked when it dawned on me that I was already halfway through my holiday, and that this time next week I would be sitting at the airport waiting to start my journey home. Would Lisa be at the airport waiting for me? I had been true to my word and not contacted her, although that had not stopped me from wondering what the future might hold for us and letting my memory wander back over that miraculous evening. It would be easy to think now that I had imagined it. But if the years in my job had taught me anything, it was that truth really is stranger than fiction. Look at Fleur's story, for instance.

And now I couldn't put it off any longer. Although thoughts of my debacle with Fleur had tickled on the edges of my mind while I'd been here, I hadn't let myself engage with it and dissect it. I hadn't put myself in therapy, so to speak. So now I pulled out a small tattered notebook from my pocket and prepared myself to jot down and name thoughts and feelings just as they came to me. This was a technique I had fallen back on sometimes with certain clients to drill down to the essence of what was going on inside their head. I remembered, poignantly, when I had just learned about it and used it for myself. It was when I was considering leaving Lisa.

I deliberately made an effort to project back over my time with Fleur, both the sessions last year and the more recent ones. I wrote down exactly what came into my head, without censoring it. I ordered a second glass of wine, which would loosen the wheels of the analytical processes, I told myself. Then I looked through my list and discarded what didn't quite fit, or what no longer fitted or what were not the most important factors. Finally I was left with two words: *Infatuation* and *embarrassed.*

My feelings around Fleur had amounted to infatuation, however you cared to define it. She and her unusual story had fascinated and attracted me, and I had allowed myself to be carried away by those emotions. I take full responsibility for that. I would have to dig even deeper to get to the bottom of why I had let that happen, but I didn't consider it was necessary to go and delve into it at the present time. The main thing was that I had ceased to be in the grip of the infatuation. I had stepped away.

Embarrassed. Perhaps embarrassment is often the hallmark of a spent infatuation, but my sensation went further than that. I was thoroughly ashamed now of my professional transgressions, including following her on the dating website. I thanked my lucky stars that Daphne had taken a leap of faith in me and made allowances for a first offence. I would take my little notebook along to my next session with her and show her my scribblings. I hoped she would be pleased with my progress. It was gratifying to get a metaphorical pat on the head from someone as rigorous as Daphne. I knew I would feel uncomfortable with the knowledge that I wasn't telling her everything. But how could I tell her about that last troubling episode, when I saw Fleur come out of her house with the Michael look-alike? I had broken my word to Daphne by even being there.

Chapter 20

Having a fantastic time here in Tenerife. Staying in a hostel in El Médano, which is a really cool little town. Met up with a group of students in the hostel and been hanging out with them. Yesterday I went with them on a bike ride up into the mountains. I kept up, no problem! Tonight it's their last night so we're taking a van into the mountains again to see the stars. See you next week, Dad.

I'd wanted to finish my message to Nathan by asking how his mum was, or sending her my love, but that would have seemed odd since I'd never done that. But I did send a couple of photos. One was of me with the group and our cycles, having a rest in a little village on the mountain slopes. The other was a selfie on the summit of Montaña Roja, with a view of the coast behind me. In both I looked tanned and healthy. That's what sunshine, exercise and a complete break from routine and problems does for you.

Nathan hadn't replied to my message, but then he often doesn't. It seems that kids don't think it impolite or even necessary to reply, or so Lisa told me. Or had he read the message and thought, Dad's a total dickhead? I read it again and it did seem a bit over the top. But then in the afternoon a reply came from him. It was a grinning emoji, whatever that meant.

It was true what I'd said, somewhat effusively, in my message. This holiday had turned out to be the best thing I could have done. I had just the right mix of company and time on my own to read, think, swim in the sea or simply lie in the sun and do nothing. I'd even got used to sharing a room and facilities with others, and the etiquette involved with that. Looking back on my life, I had gone straight from school to university with the intention of taking a gap year to travel when I graduated. But then Lisa had got pregnant and we got married, so it didn't happen. I missed out on all those carefree, rite-of-passage things.

But then, so did she.

Now that I was distanced from it, I was trying to stand back and take a more rational view of my impulsive suggestion to Lisa that we should give our relationship another try. I didn't feel quite so certain about it now as I first had, but what was emerging from my groping thoughts and emotions was that I had never stopped caring for her. Although on the one hand I was trying to play devil's advocate and look for reasons why we shouldn't get back together, there were pretty compelling reasons why we should. We got on well, there were the two boys, I could make her life easier by us living together and I could make up for earlier years. And, quite simply, I loved her.

I only had a couple of days left of my holiday, and it was on my conscience that there was something I hadn't done. So, should it be email or WhatsApp? Email, because it would make it seem more formal. I took my phone out and wrote the first couple of words, *Dear Cora*. Now what? Who was I writing this for, me or her? My finger hovered over the screen. Then without further procrastination I went for it:

It's taken me a bit of time to write to you, but here goes. First of all, how are you? I have heard that your exhibition was a huge success, and I'm glad. You deserve it.

So, what can I say? What I did by not turning up to your event was despicable. Despicable and cowardly. I did have something, a work thing, that I'd got involved with on that afternoon and I didn't realise the time, but that's no excuse. I should have checked. Part of it is that I've always found your work, your art, difficult because I don't understand it and I feel out of my depth. Yet I know it's a central part of who you are, and from what other people say – not my own poor judgement! – I understand you're good at it.

And, if I'm totally honest I think our relationship had gone past its best. We'd got into a rut and we weren't going forward. For instance, neither of us wanted to move in together, or become part of each other's friends and family. But let me say, I thought we had tremendous fun, and tremendous sex. I wouldn't have missed it.

As I said, all this is no excuse for me. I wish you good luck and good things, Cora.

Simon x

When I pressed 'send' it was coming up to six o'clock, which is when we were heading off for this stargazing business. I wondered how long it would take Cora to look at the email, and if she would reply. If she did, it probably wouldn't be until tomorrow. But I was wrong. Her reply came back five minutes later. She must hardly have had time to read it, I thought as I opened it.

You're an arsehole

I turned the phone off and went to get a sweater for the evening. Closure? I suppose.

*

I wasn't sure if I was that enthusiastic about another excursion up into the mountains just to look at the night sky, but it was friendly of them to have asked me so I'd accepted. They'd filled the minivan with people from the hostel, including Sven and Lars and others whom I hadn't met. David was at the wheel and we wound our way upwards into the hinterland until we came to a roadside bar where we could eat and wait for the sun to go down.

'Come and sit by me, King of the Mountains!' said Liam. I felt myself glow with pleasure at the Tour de France reference. I'd been able to keep up with the leaders on the cycle ride, men more than ten years younger than me, although it had been quite tough on the relentless slopes.

'Cycle a lot, do you?' he said. 'You're really good.'

I said with offhand modesty that I had cycled for as long as

I could remember and that nowadays I was out every Sunday with a cycling club. It felt good to impress them.

Darkness had fallen when we all piled back into the van to travel further up the slopes, and already we could see the stars glimmering at us. The plan was to travel towards the top of the mountain and pull in to a lay-by to view the night sky in all its glory. Apparently Mount Teide in Tenerife is one of the very best stargazing spots in the world, because of the lack of light pollution. You can pick out constellations if you know what you're looking for. I didn't. I can't say that astronomy has ever been one of my interests although, like most people, I think the stars are nice enough. It was a total surprise to me, therefore, when I stepped out of the van at our high vantage point and the sky was like I'd never imagined it could be. Certainly it wasn't like this where I lived. It was crowded with more stars than seemed possible. They looked much brighter, too. It blew me away.

I moved away from the rest of the group, who were exclaiming and pointing, and lay down on my back to look up at the dome of the sky above me. I could feel the earth cold and solid against my back as it supported me. Now I'm not religious or anything, and I've heard plenty about, and from, people who have had sublime experiences, but for a couple of minutes all that existed was just the earth below me, the sky above me, and me. Nothing else mattered. Yes, I've made some mistakes, but I'm human. I've learned from them. Would Lisa decide to work towards us becoming a couple again? I don't know. And in the grand scheme of things, it didn't matter.

'Lying down is a great idea. I was getting quite a crick in my neck.' It was Poppy's voice in my ear, as she lay down beside me. 'Isn't this the most magnificent experience you've ever had?'

'Mmm. It's certainly one of them.'

'One of them? What have you seen that's been more amazing than this?'

'Well… seeing my son born is up there as amazing, on my

173

scale.' I could still recall the rush of pure love I had felt when I had first looked into Nathan's unfocused eyes as Lisa held him; a little helpless replica of us, with all the joy and pain ahead of him. Suddenly I felt melancholy.

'Yeah, I guess I concede that. Surely it's different though, isn't it? A birth is hugely personal whereas all these planets and galaxies up there… well, it's just the opposite. It's all been there for countless millennia and it just carries on the same, no matter what happens down here.'

I said I knew what she meant and we watched in silence for a while. I was glad that I'd brought extra clothing.

I heard her turn her head towards me. 'You must be divorced, right? Only you don't have any family in tow.'

'Yes, I'm divorced. One of the many, unfortunately. I miss my son. Oh, I see him quite often, but I've lost out on being in his life on a day-to-day basis.'

Poppy slipped her hand into mine and squeezed it. What a nice kid she was. 'But then, there's all these stars,' she said.

I heard the trudge of footsteps next to us. It was Jessica coming to tell us that they were about to head off and there would be drinks on the beach when we got back to mark the last night.

*

The beach felt pleasantly mild after the much cooler temperatures of the mountains. The group was more subdued tonight, which was probably the effect of the stargazing. Even so, after half an hour of drinking and chatting I felt the urge to break away and be by myself. I walked a little way down the beach and sat on the sand, looking out into the darkness and sipping from my bottle of beer. The muted sound of the waves on the shore was soporific. I was just contemplating calling it a night and going to bed when I saw Poppy heading towards me holding two bottles of beer, her spiky short hair and jaunty step easily recognisable.

'I saw you'd gone off on your own so I thought I'd join you in case you were, you know, a bit sad. Don't mind, do you?' She passed me one of the bottles. I hesitated then took it. I didn't really want any more to drink, but it was thoughtful of her to see if I was OK.

'That's really kind of you. I'm fine though. To see my son only on an occasional basis is a way of life. I don't know why I said anything.'

'Probably the effect of that incredible sky. It was, like, awesome.'

I agreed. 'Are you looking forward to going home? The new term will start soon, won't it?' I wanted to change the subject.

'I suppose I'm looking forward to it. It'll be cool to see my friends.' We both swigged our beer while I asked about her course at university and we chatted for a while. She had taken off her sandals and was wiggling her toes in the sand. Suddenly she said, 'You know, you're really nice.'

I didn't know how I was supposed to respond to this. 'So are you,' I said, somewhat guardedly. I wasn't sure where this was going.

She moved her naked foot over and laid it on top of mine. Even in the low light I could see the wink of her toenails, painted some garish colour, and I could feel the sensuous movements of her foot. 'The other two girls who were sharing the room with Jessica and me went home this afternoon, so it's empty right now. Jessica's with the others and I've asked her not to come in until I text her. Oh, and she won't tell Liam because he'd go mental.'

There was not a hint of shyness or even flirting about her. I didn't know if this demonstration was a front or she really was this bold. Either way, there was no doubt about what she meant.

I had absolutely not seen this coming. 'Poppy…' I withdrew my foot and stumbled over what to say next.

'You did say you were divorced, didn't you? And I assume you don't have a girlfriend or she would either be with you or you'd have talked about her.'

She'd got it all sorted out alright, in her brisk manner. I didn't know whether to feel flattered that she fancied me, or targeted and preyed upon. An interesting change of gender roles, my professional head said.

'You're right, I don't have a girlfriend. Our relationship broke up a few days before I came here.'

'Then you need a bit of consoling. And after tomorrow we'll never see each other again.' She smiled at me without guile and took my hand.

'How old are you, Poppy?'

'Twenty.'

'My son will be fifteen in a couple of weeks. Also I'm old enough to be your father, just about.'

She shrugged, still smiling. 'So? What does that matter?' It was simple to her.

I groaned. 'Look, my life has been a bit of a mess lately, which is the real reason why I'm here on my own. But a wonderful thing happened just before I came away, which is that there's a chance my ex-wife and I might get back together again, and I can't risk doing anything to blow that.'

I expected her to brush my reservations to one side and carry on regardless with her aggressive seduction, but instead she sat back and said, 'Wow. You might make it up with your wife? That's immense. How did it happen?'

I found myself telling her a shortened version of my relationship with Lisa, and how we'd unexpectedly had a night of drunken passion together. She was round-eyed with interest, interrupting me to ask questions now and again.

'I think that's just the most amazing thing I've ever heard,' she said. 'Oh, I do hope it all works out for you. It's so romantic.'

The suddenly she sighed and buried her face in her hands. When I asked her what was wrong she lifted her head and I saw she was crying. She said, 'I wish my parents could have got back together. I used to pray for that every night. That was until I realised it was never going to happen.'

So it ended up with her telling me the story of her parents' divorce and its effect on her and her brother, and me listening. It's what I do, after all.

*

The Departure Lounge was packed with holidaymakers, most of them looking tanned and rested, like me. When I'd looked in the mirror that morning, I'd hardly recognised myself, I looked so chilled. I'd got to the airport in plenty of time; once through security there was about an hour until we boarded. I was not sorry to be going home, both because the holiday had served its purpose and also because yesterday a lot of new people had checked into the hostel. They were younger and altogether noisier and rowdier than the guys I had got to know. The genial Swedes in my room had been replaced by a loutish pair of Brits, so the earplugs came in useful. I never knew what happened to the older Spanish guy. It seemed I was leaving at just the right time.

I pulled out my work mobile and switched it on. I hadn't been going to bring it with me on holiday, because I'd had no intention of looking at anything to do with work. However it had occurred to me that if anything had happened to my own phone, it would be good to have a back-up. There was only one message, and it was from Kai:

Hi mate, it's all happening here. Neville has disappeared. Done a bunk. Fill you in when you get back. Hope you're having fun. Maybe you got lucky?? K

I stared at the screen and wondered what it was all about. Disappeared? That sounded dramatic. As for getting lucky, I wasn't going to boast to Kai about my being hit on by an attractive twenty-year-old. He'd never credit it that I'd turned her

177

down. Even leaving aside the Lisa angle, her full-on approach was a bit of a turn-off to me. I liked to be the one who did the chasing. Yes, she was vivacious and attractive, but let's face it, Nathan would be seeing girls like her before long. Still, she *had* fancied me. Me, boring old Simon. I let myself linger over that thought again.

I looked at my watch. There was time before we boarded to phone Kai, if he was around, and get the dirt on this thing about Neville. I was frankly curious.

'Kai?'

'Hiya mate. You home already?' There was indistinct background noise, like the chinking of crockery.

'No, I'm at the airport in Tenerife, waiting to board the plane. But listen, what's all this cryptic stuff about Neville?'

'Oh, that. No-one seems to know the full story, but it seems that he's been caught out in some malpractice with a woman client. Serious stuff, I gather. And there's rumours that he had his hand in the till at his last place. Now he's cleared off, and that tells you he's guilty, doesn't it? I can't say I ever liked him.'

'Did anyone?' I said as I tried to take in this bombshell. Kai summarised such details as he knew. Then he said, 'Now his job's available, of course. And people are mentioning your name. What do you think?'

I laughed, as you do when you want to cover your feelings. 'Oh, we'll have to see about that.'

'Well, just giving you the heads-up. Anyway, how was your holiday?' I heard a female voice and Kai saying that he'd come and get it in a minute.

I told him the holiday was fantastic and that I'd make him jealous with my tan. I didn't want to keep him from his late breakfast and from the woman who had presumably cooked it, so I left it at that.

As we were saying goodbye the first call came for preboarding my flight. There was a flurry of activity around me as people gathered up their bags, checked their documents and jostled to get a place in the queue for the plane. I stayed still in my seat, phone in hand. I was one of the last people to board.

*

As the plane gained height we flew directly over El Médano and I saw clearly the shape of the coast and the town, with Montaña Roja standing guard over it all. Good bye, El Médano. Will I ever come back? Probably not. It was enchanting and fun, but maybe it had served its purpose for me. El Médano had been a fitting place to let go of Fleur. Whatever happened now between her and her Michael-replacement, and what went on in her head, wasn't my business. It never had been, apart from the hours in The Willows when she had paid for it to be my business. Perhaps I would tell Daphne everything after all. And then the file would be totally closed.

I spent the four-hour journey reading, dozing and idly drifting back to the turmoil I had felt when I was on the outward journey, compared to how I felt now. I would slot myself into my life again, into the job I loved. This time tomorrow I would be at work where no doubt everyone would be talking about what had happened while I was away. There had been no message from Lisa, so I assumed she wouldn't be meeting me at the airport. Well, it had been a big, and impulsive, ask. I would contact her in a couple of days and we'd see where we stood. Whatever happened next, we had become closer and that had to be good for the boys.

The plane landed on time. We all went through the palaver of shuffling off, queueing for immigration, finding the correct baggage carousel and waiting patiently for your luggage to be disgorged. I could have put my slightly elevated heartbeat down to the fact that it's always stressful to be waiting for your bag to appear. What if it doesn't? It had never happened to me, but it's possible. I flicked my phone on. The signal had re-established itself after being in flight mode, but there were no messages.

There was still a lot of people standing around waiting when my scruffy backpack appeared, looking incongruous amongst all the uniform, sleek suitcases. I grabbed it and headed for the Arrivals Hall.

There was the usual gaggle of people on the other side of the barrier. Some were holding up placards with names on, while others waved excitedly when they saw their loved ones emerge. I was considering whether I should queue for the bus or splash out on a taxi, when Joe came running out of the crowd towards me. He threw his arms around my waist in one of his bear hugs.

It was enough.